DISCOVERED LIAISONS

DISCOVERED LIAISONS

THE DISCOVERED TRUTH SERIES ROMANTIC SUSPENSE
BOOK FOUR

JULIE BAWDEN DAVIS

Roses ARE RED PUBLISHING

ACKNOWLEDGMENTS

As they say, it takes a village. Here's my village. I'm supremely grateful to each of these fabulous people!

ARC Reading Gems
Julie Schlueter
Mandy Stanley
Tara Bradley
Angela Barnes
Heather Wamboldt

Pros
Sharon Whatley, editing
Judy Bullard, cover design
Kayla Curry, logo design
Kyle Kane, logo design
Sabrina Wildermuth, design consultation
Jeremy Davis, book design

To my stepfather, Bill, the best forensic auditor and father. You are greatly missed.

Jessica Reynolds stopped staring at the spreadsheet on the computer and closed her eyes. The numbers weren't matching up, and she had to balance the client's profit and loss statement. She wanted to go home. Her kitty, Natalia, needed to be fed. But her boss, Anthony, had made it clear. Balance tonight, or don't come in tomorrow.

Opening her eyes, she decided to take another go at it, when a fraud alert popped up on her email. She skimmed the email, then went into her credit protection account. Sure enough, someone had accessed her social security number. As her blood pressure rose and her heart rate increased, she checked several other reports. How could this be happening? As a forensic auditor for a high-profile accounting firm, Jessica had helped enough people exposed to identity theft to know this was a disaster in the making.

She checked her other data protection account that scanned the dark web. Sure enough, it also showed her social had been accessed within the last twenty-four hours. Her mind whirled. What would she do if this was a client? Track down the source, of course.

Jessica spent the next thirty minutes performing an audit of her own accounts. After some cyber sleuthing, she located the IP address of the computer that had retrieved her social. What on earth? She'd never even been to Mexico. Further digging led her to Puerto Vallarta.

Jessica tapped on her desk blotter with her pen. It wouldn't be long before the person who stole her social ruined her credit entirely. She had to stop this in its tracks.

Jessica went online and booked the next flight out of Dulles to Puerto Vallarta. It left at five in the morning. That gave her a couple of hours still to get things together.

She dialed her boss's number. Straight to voicemail. Not surprising, since it was midnight. She waited for the tone.

"Hi Anthony, I've got a little problem. Really, a big problem. Someone has stolen my social. The point of origin is Puerto Vallarta, Mexico. I'm flying there tonight to get this sorted out. I will, um, work more on that one case while I'm on the road."

She rushed out of the accounting office to her apartment in Georgetown, dialing her friend Meg's number as she exited the elevator and made her way out the front door of the Washington DC high-rise where she worked.

"Jess, it's late. You okay?"

"Q Street in Georgetown," she told the taxi driver as she climbed in. "Hi, Meg, sorry. Can you do me a big favor? I need someone to watch Natalia for a few days. I've got to go to Puerto Vallarta."

"Tell me you're going on a last-minute trip to paradise with a hot guy."

"Not quite. It's a financial thing."

"That's a long way from home."

"I'll explain when I get back. I have plenty of food for Natalia, and litter. If you can stop by in the morning that'd be great."

"Have fun for me," said Meg.

Jessica agreed and hung up the phone as the driver stopped in front of her apartment. She walked the few short steps to the door of her Victorian brownstone. As soon as she opened the door, Natalia greeted her. Jessica picked up the white angora beauty and buried her face in her fur.

"Hi there, gorgeous. Mommy's home to feed you, but I have some news you're not going to like."

Spencer Abbott smiled as he clicked his computer off and stood to stretch. Three days from now he'd be in Aspen. Skiing, and hopefully not alone. He'd just finished consulting in the Far East for nearly a month for the Secret Service, untangling a counterfeit ring. Time for some hearty soup by a warm fire in Aspen's cool, crisp air.

His phone rang and he glanced at the caller ID. Anthony Thompson, his college buddy. He hadn't heard from him in quite a while.

"What's up, Anthony?"

"I need a favor. I've got this employee. A genius when it comes to forensic auditing, but she's not used to being in the field. I think she's walking into some trouble, and I can't get ahold of her. Her phone's off. She's my best forensic auditor, and I can't risk anything happening to her."

"How can I help?"

"Can you meet up with her in Puerto Vallarta where she's headed? Someone has stolen her social security number. It shouldn't take more than two days tops. I'd compensate you handsomely."

Spencer thought about his friend's request. Mexico wasn't one of his favorite places, but the money would come in handy at the resort in Aspen. He could maybe upgrade to a penthouse suite.

"Give me her name and cell phone number. I'll have one of my buddies trace it when she turns it back on. No worries."

Jessica buckled her seat belt, then placed her handbag on the floor, pulling out some gum. Glancing about, she noticed a man eyeing her from the other side of the airplane's aisle. His dark good looks made her stare more than she intended. He was talking on the phone with someone and didn't acknowledge her; just studied her. She reached into her bag again and pulled out her computer tablet. Maybe she could fit in time after all to work on that case for her boss. Best to keep her mind occupied so she didn't start imagining disastrous scenarios about her stolen social security number.

Once Spencer settled on the flight to Puerto Vallarta, he called his contact at the Secret Service, who pinged the woman's cell phone. Spencer couldn't believe his good luck when he was informed that the owner of the phone was just a few feet away from him. In addition to winding up sitting near her on the same flight to Puerto Vallarta, she was gorgeous.

As he watched her, Spencer wondered if Anthony had something going on with his best auditor, even though he was married. Not the sort of scenario Spencer would ever personally involve himself in, but he had to admit the job suddenly got a lot more interesting.

When the stewardess announced they were twenty minutes from Puerto Vallarta, Jessica stretched and yawned. She had dozed off a couple hours after takeoff, frustrated that she now had another problem to deal with. She hadn't been able to balance the client's P & L report for her boss yet. Hopefully, she had better luck tracking down her social security number.

Making sure her cell phone was still in the seatback in front of her, she got up and took her purse to the bathroom. A little water on her face and a fresh coat of lipstick would make her feel more awake. When she passed the man who had been looking at her earlier, she peeked at him. He appeared to be sleeping.

When Jessica left for the bathroom, Spencer finally had the chance to slip a tracker into her phone. But how to pull that off without attracting attention from the woman sitting next to her? Fortunately, she also got up. He rose quickly and crossed the aisle, gesturing for her to pass in front of him.

The woman smiled, sidled out of the seats, and made her way toward the back of the plane. Spencer pretended to drop something, in case anyone else was watching, and reached down and grabbed Jessica's phone. Working quickly, he slipped in the tracker and snapped the phone shut, shoving it back in the seat pocket. Then he casually sat back down in his seat.

When the plane set down in Puerto Vallarta, it was eleven in the morning and eighty-five degrees. Jessica welcomed the warm weather. It had been cold for months in DC. Maybe she could spend a couple extra days here working from the hotel room, soaking up the warmth and checking out the area. That adventurous thought made her feel a ripple of excitement. Meg was always telling her that she lived a boring, protected life and to take some chances. Maybe this was the place to do that.

Jessica made her way down the airplane's stairs as the balmy air greeted her. She admired the palm trees next to the airport's main terminal swaying in the slight breeze. In the distance, she spotted green mountains covered with jungle terrain.

Back in DC, she had pinpointed the general area where her social security number was being used, so she grabbed a cab, instructing the driver to head to a hotel in that area. When she walked into the hotel's foyer a few minutes later, Jessica admired the floor to ceiling windows on the far wall showcasing an open-air atrium bursting with lush, green vegetation readily growing in the tropical climate. In the center of the scene was a tall, multi-layered fountain lazily splashing water. As she stared at the tranquil scene, the fatigue from not sleeping fully last night hit her. Sometimes a few candy bars and black coffee could wake her back up, but she knew that wasn't going to be enough right now. Marching up to the front desk where a pert Latina woman stood ready to help, she announced, "I'd like a room."

"For one or two?" asked the woman.

"One," said Jessica, taking out her credit card.

"How many nights?"

Jessica hesitated. "That's somewhat open-ended. Is that a problem?"

"Well, we have a convention coming in at the end of the week…"

"Okay, put me down for three days for now."

The woman nodded and clicked away on the computer, as Jessica's eyelids drooped. She would be getting to her room in the nick of time, it looked like. What did her Aunt Emmaline back in Ohio always say? A tired mind is a nuisance, but a rested mind can move mountains. She'd get some rest so she could wake up and move some mountains. As she headed for the elevator, room key in hand, she thought she felt someone watching her. Jessica turned around, but there was no one else in the lobby.

Sliding the keycard into her room door a few minutes later, Jessica pushed it open and dumped her things at the foot of the bed. Peeling off her blouse and pants, she pulled back the covers and slid in between the soft sheets. Laying her head on the down pillow, she soon felt herself drifting off to sleep. Just a little nap before she stopped the identity thief from ruining her life.

3

Spencer checked the time. He'd been watching Jessica's door for two hours. No one in and no one out. Maybe she wasn't in there alone. As far as Spencer was concerned, bringing Anthony the news that his girlfriend was cheating on him still deserved full payment.

Movement behind Spencer caused him to turn. The maid.

"*Hola*," he said and smiled at the older woman, who pushed a cart stacked high with towels and toiletry items.

"*Señor*, you need help?"

"No, just waiting for my girlfriend." Spencer nodded at Jessica's door.

The maid smiled, took a stack of towels from her cart, and started for the door.

"I wouldn't go in there." Spencer warned her. "My girlfriend is upset about her hair."

The maid looked at the door, unsure.

Spencer reached out for the towels. "I'm happy to give them to her." As he did so, he knocked a stack of toilet paper from the cart. The rolls scattered on the floor.

"Forgive me! Let me help you pick that up."

Once the items were retrieved, Spencer reached in his pocket and took out a wad of bills. The woman's eyebrows raised.

"No, *gracias, Señor.*"

"I insist," he said, laying a ten-dollar bill into her hand.

"*Muchas gracias.*" She smiled at him.

"*De nada,*" said Spencer.

She bustled to the next room and rapped on the door, calling out "housekeeping" to the occupants. When they answered, she gathered a stack of towels and made her way into the room.

Spencer used the master keycard he had borrowed from the maid and slid it into Jessica's door. The light turned green, and he slipped inside. No couple rolling around in the bed, but the shower was on.

He set the towels down on the bureau and went over to a chair next to the window and took a seat. After a bit, he peeked through the venetian blinds to the garden below. There was a small maze just like the one at his childhood home in Veracruz.

"She's nothing but a Mexican trollop!" His English grandmother hissed to his father while visiting. "I know she's the boy's mother, but you're an Abbott. The family business needs you." Spencer was six at the time, and they were standing in what his mother called the garden room, which looked out at the back yard.

"Quiet down, mother, the boy is listening."

"It's about time he knew the truth."

"Let me talk to Angelica. I don't think it's a good idea to take him out of school right now. He just adjusted."

"The schools in England are far superior to Mexican schools. What you mean is you don't want to separate the boy from his mother."

"You've made it clear my wife isn't welcome in England."

"We've never said such a thing."

"She can tell, plus she won't leave Mexico."

"Figure this out, son. You have an obligation."

Spencer ran out of the garden room to hide in the maze.

The bathroom door opened, and Spencer sat up in the chair. Jessica came out alone, wrapped in a too-big white robe that engulfed her. When she started to scream, Spencer leapt across the room, grabbing her by the waist with one hand and wrapping his other hand across her mouth.

Her blue eyes filled with terror.

"I'm not here to hurt you," he said lowly and evenly. She smelled fresh scrubbed. "I was sent by Anthony Thompson." Her eyes calmed a bit at the name. "I am going to remove my hand from your mouth, but it's very important you don't scream. If you do, I'll have to gag you."

She nodded her head, so he removed his hand slowly and she began shaking. The feel of her fear tugged at him. But he was just doing his job, he told himself.

"Why don't you sit down, and I'll explain," he said more gently than he'd heard himself speak in years. He gestured for her to sit in the chair he had vacated.

She sat down and looked back at him. He liked the natural beauty of her—the smooth, radiant skin free of makeup, her blond hair, long and glossy.

"Will someone be here soon, Jessica?" he asked.

"What, who?"

The look in her eyes told Spencer that his presumptions had been wrong. Could it be that she really was here about a stolen social security number?

Jessica struggled to make sense of the man standing over her. He said he had come at the request of her boss. But why had he broken into her hotel room? And was this a ruse? Had he somehow gotten her boss's name and was really here to hurt her?

"What do you want?" Jessica finally managed to say in a surer tone than she felt.

"My name is Spencer Abbott, and I am a friend of Anthony's. He was concerned for your safety, so he sent me to watch over you. You aren't here with anyone else?"

Jessica sat up straighter, the shock at being surprised in her room being replaced with annoyance.

"If you're referring to the someone who stole my social security number, that's why I'm here. Otherwise, I have no idea what you're talking about. And furthermore, did Mr. Thompson give you permission to break into my hotel room while you were watching over me?"

Spencer waited a moment before he spoke.

"Look. I understand that someone stole your social security number. I'm here to help you deal with the issue. That's all. Me entering your room, it was just a precaution."

"A precaution? You couldn't have simply knocked on the door?"

"Identity thieves don't play around," said Spencer.

"I work in forensic auditing. Our company does outside audits for government agencies, and I've testified in court. My work has taken down identity theft rings. I think I know a serious matter. That's why I took the next plane out when I figured out where my social security number was being used."

"Anthony told me you are an expert auditor. My job is to provide protection, and that's exactly what I'm doing. Might be a little harsh, but my methods, they get the job done."

"Tell Mr. Thompson thank you, but I don't need a bodyguard. You can leave now."

Spencer wasn't about to get on the next plane out after making a commitment to Anthony. But fine, he'd leave her room—for now. Before doing so, he grabbed her phone from the table. When she started to protest, he said, "I was hired to watch out for you." He tapped his number into her phone and saved it, then handed it back to her. "Call me when you need me."

Spencer walked out and shut the door after himself and stood outside of the room for a moment. This job, including Jessica, was going to be a challenge, he thought. And he hadn't had a good challenge in a long time.

4

Jessica opened her laptop. Pinpointing the exact location of the IP address where her social security number had been compromised would take some time. But after digging for a couple of hours, while munching on French fries and a burger from room service, she found it. A bar in downtown Puerto Vallarta.

Donning a pair of black slacks and a short-sleeved navy-blue blouse, she swept her blond hair back in a barrette. Then she grabbed her purse and slipped out of her hotel room. She half expected to see that man hovering around her doorway, but he was blessedly gone.

In the hotel lobby, she grabbed a map of downtown, then headed out. As she walked to the bar, she passed street vendors with poster boards onto which they'd pinned colorful scarves and attached costume jewelry. She soon discovered that if she stopped to admire the colorful garb, or even made eye contact, the vendors became eager, and some even followed her. At one point, a bright red tour bus passed by, emitting the scent of diesel fuel.

When she arrived at the bar, she was greeted by cigarette smoke and beer, and the dim space pulsated with Spanish pop music. She hated the smell of smoke and tried to resist fanning the haze in front of her.

The bar was full of men and a smattering of scantily dressed women.

The stares from the men and glares from the women unsettled her. She steeled her shoulders as a man approached her.

"*Chica*," he said. His breath smelled of alcohol, and his eyes glinted in an unfriendly way that sent a slither of unease down her spine. "What can we do to help you?"

"The bathroom. *El baño?*" she asked.

"Back there," he motioned with his head.

Jessica walked toward the rear of the room where he'd pointed, forcing herself not to look back to see if he followed. When she arrived in front of a door with a skirt painted on it, she glanced back at him. He had turned away.

Jessica continued down the hallway, stopping when she came to a door that read *oficina*. She pushed it open and entered. There was the computer. If she could just find and erase her social security number, she will have solved the problem. Breathing shallowly and hands shaking, she typed in her social. It popped up, along with a string of other social security numbers. She hit delete. Just as she finished, she heard voices coming down the hallway. Her heart lurched into her throat as she spotted a broom closet and ran over to squeeze her way into it.

Peeking out of a crack in the door, she saw two men enter the room. One was the man from the front of the bar. The other man was short with a thick neck, and he held an envelope.

"No one can trace them back to you? Boss lady wants me to make sure."

"No, way, *amigo*," said the man she first encountered. "Besides, these are all the way from *Los Estados Unidos*. No one is going to be looking for their social *seguridades* here." He began tapping the keys on the computer, a confused expression clouding his face.

The beefy man appeared impatient. "*Rapido, amigo*, I need to get back."

The barman turned the computer off and back on, becoming even more agitated. "*No entiendo!* The numbers aren't here."

"The numbers are gone?"

"No one comes back here."

"You're telling me someone got on to your computer?"

"No, it must be some sort of virus."

"We can't take that chance. Sorry, *amigo*." Jessica's hands flew to her mouth when he pulled out a gun and lifting it to the man's forehead, pulled the trigger. The gun apparently had a silencer, because it made very little sound. Then he put the envelope and gun in his pockets and left the room.

Shaking in places she didn't know could shake, Jessica waited to see if anyone else was coming. When it remained quiet, she opened the closet door and stepped out, nearly tripping over the dead man's legs. Except for funerals, she'd never seen a dead body. Feeling trapped and breathless at the sight, she grabbed the door handle, pulling it open and rushing out into the hallway. When a strong hand grabbed her arm, she felt her legs go weak.

"Tell me you did what you needed to do," said Spencer.

"Something went terribly wrong."

"What?" He looked in her eyes, and then reached out and flung the door open, revealing the dead man sprawled on the floor in a pool of blood. "Bloody hell! We need to get out of here."

"It wasn't me. I—."

Suddenly, one of the women who had been glaring at her in the bar was heading straight toward them.

"Hey!" she called out.

Spencer pulled Jessica with him down the hall. Just when they reached the back door, the woman screamed, "Enrique, *Dios mío!*"

Spencer grabbed the door handle to swing it open, but it was bolted from the inside. "Watch out," he told Jessica, pushing her behind him, then shooting the doorknob. The bullet knocked the knob out, at which point he kicked the door open. "Run for your life, Jessica, and don't stop until I tell you," he ordered as they sped down the street and crossed through the promenade.

Once they got to a sidewalk swarming with people, Spencer slowed his pace. "We're going to attract attention if we continue to run," he said, pulling her close to him as they made their way down the sidewalk. "Give me your cell phone."

Jessica pulled the phone out of her coat pocket. Spencer grabbed the phone and powered it down. "Your phone can't be tracked, as long as it stays off," he told her.

As they walked, Spencer's mind raced. Chances were, the authorities wouldn't link Jessica to the crime right away. It was probably okay to go back to the hotel room and get her stuff—but quickly. He didn't say anything while they walked. Once inside her room with the door shut, he turned to her and spoke.

"What the hell happened there?"

Jessica explained while Spencer listened intently.

"Did you wear gloves?"

"I didn't think…. Oh, God, what am I going to do?"

"Your fingerprints may not be in any databases, unless you've been arrested."

"No, never arrested." Jessica shook her head, but then her eyes flew open. "We work on government contracts at the accounting office. I have top secret clearance."

"Shit!" Spencer spat out, hitting the hotel desk with his fist and making Jessica jump.

"You're scaring me," she said.

"You should be scared."

5

Jessica watched Spencer strum his fingers on the edge of the desk.

"I suppose you used your credit card when you checked into the hotel," he said finally.

Jessica didn't want to answer. She realized only now how stupid she'd been, leaving a digital trail wherever she went. In fact, what was she thinking coming here to Mexico in the first place on a one-woman crusade?

Spencer sighed. "I'll take your silence as a yes." He glanced around the room. "We need to get out of here. Did you bring any cash with you?"

"A couple of hundred, and then I planned on using credit cards."

"That'll help. I've got some cash. When you check out, pay cash and ask that they don't run your card. If they want to keep your card in the system in case of damages, then I'll create a diversion, so you can wipe it from their system.

Jessica opened her mouth to protest, but Spencer stopped her. "Anthony says you're a genius on the computer. You'll need to do this quickly."

She nodded, then got up and gathered her things. Her hands were shaking as she put her toiletries in a bag. What a mess this had become, she thought. Taking a deep breath, she headed out of the bathroom, depositing the bag and her computer in her carry-on. She motioned to pick it up, but Spencer grabbed it. She was about to protest and insist she could carry her own bag but decided to save her energy for something more important.

"Thank you," she said.

Spencer watched Jessica's face, and something tugged at him. It wasn't her flawless beauty, though that was admittedly nice to look at, it was a pureness and a genuineness about her. She meant what she said, and he hadn't seen that often in his life.

"I'm getting paid for my trouble, no need to thank me," he said more dismissively than he intended before turning and heading out the hotel room door.

Down at the front desk, Jessica paid in cash and asked the attendant to take her credit card out of the system. As Spencer had predicted, the hotel employee said he needed to keep it in until the room was checked out.

"Perhaps you could have someone go up and check?" she said. "I didn't mean to give you that card. It's going to expire soon, and I don't have the new one."

"Do you have another card, *señorita*?" asked the employee.

"No, I don't, I—"

Just then a giant vase on a table at the other side of the large foyer crashed to the floor. The young man looked up in shock, and said, "Excuse me." He ran toward the commotion.

Jessica took the opportunity to slip behind the desk and sighed in relief when she saw the screen with her credit card information was up. She changed three digits on her card number and her last name to Ronalds, then hit save. Scrambling back, she repositioned herself on the other side of the desk.

"What a shame about that beautiful vase," she said when the young man returned, flustered.

"Yes, the owner won't be pleased. No one seems to know how it happened." He peered at the screen. "Did you say you had another card?"

"You know what, that card should be good, after all. Sorry for the confusion."

The young man looked bewildered as she spun on her heels and headed for the hotel's front door.

Once outside, she saw Spencer waiting by a taxi at the curb. He ushered her into the vehicle, then slid in himself.

"Where to, *Señor*?" asked the taxi driver.

"To the airport."

"Wait a minute." Jessica whispered in Spencer's ear. "I need to find out who has my social security number. That's why I came."

"You said you wiped the computer in the bar clean."

"But I can't be sure he didn't transmit the information. And what about the person who sold it? Also, I just erased my social from that computer. Someone who knows computers would be able to retrieve it."

"You have much bigger problems right now."

Jessica sat back in her seat and sighed. Maybe he was right. She might be better off getting out of here away from the murder and trying to mitigate the damage from home.

By the time they pulled up to the airport, she had already planned to triangulate some data and track down any IP addresses associated with the dead guy's computer. As they were about to get out of the taxi, Jessica spied the guy who had shot the man in the bar. She pulled on Spencer's arm as he motioned to exit the cab.

"It's him. The man with the gun in the bar," she hissed.

Spencer's eyebrows raised. "Change of plans, *amigo*," he said to the cab driver. "I must have looked at the tickets wrong. Our flight doesn't leave until tomorrow. Do you know any place in the countryside? Somewhere out of the way, where my *novia* and I can get a little privacy?"

The man looked back at Spencer in the rearview mirror and replied in stilted English, "My uncle has a little hotel in Yelapa. It is about forty minutes from here."

"Perfect," said Spencer, putting his arm around Jessica and pulling her close.

Though Spencer's embrace initially startled her, she felt oddly comforted by him. He had a certain energy about him that had a way of lulling her.

As they rode along, Jessica wondered how long before she'd be able to go home. The thought reminded her of her cat waiting for her return. "I need to call my friend Meg," she exclaimed. "She's watching Natalia. May I have my phone?"

Spencer didn't respond. Who in the hell was Natalia? Did she have a kid? That was something Anthony hadn't bothered to tell him. Even more important to get her home as safely and quickly as possible.

"If you use the phone for a minute, they can trace it. You know that," replied Spencer.

"You're right. Forget it. This flying under the radar is going to take some getting used to. I'm sure Meg will take good care of her. I left plenty of food and litter."

When they arrived in Yelapa, which the driver informed them was a small fishing village surrounded by jungle terrain that his family had called home for decades, night had fallen. A neon sign in front of the hotel said *vacancia*.

"At least they have room," Spencer commented, reaching into his pocket and removing a hundred. He handed it to the driver and said, "We'd prefer it if no one else knows we're here." The driver nodded and headed in before them, pocketing the bill.

They walked under an ivy-covered trellis and into a tiny office with a black-and-white television blaring a Mexican soap opera. A man with a goatee and paunch belly sat at the desk eating his evening meal—tortillas and beans. He rose with a big grin on his face when he saw the driver. They hugged, speaking briefly.

"*Hola*, my nephew tells me you want a romantic room, eh?" He grinned and winked at Spencer. "I have the honeymoon suite for you! The best room in *la casa!*" He lifted a key from the wall and handed it to Spencer. "It's the bungalow in the back—away from the road. Good privacy."

"*Gracias, Señor.*" Spencer put his arm around Jessica again and guided her out of the front office, leaving the two to their family reunion. Once out of their sight, he pulled away, and they made their way to the only bungalow at the back of the property. Slipping the key in, he motioned for Jessica to enter and followed her in. Then he locked the deadbolt and pulled the drapes closed.

The place consisted of a large bedroom, sitting area with a couch, a mini kitchen and bathroom. Spencer set her carry-on bag by the bed.

"Why don't you get some rest? I'll take the couch," he suggested. He sat down on the cushions and watched as she opened her bag. That's when he spied it. He blinked and shook his head, but it was still there.

6

Jessica flipped the top closed on her bag, but she was too late. Spencer was behind her in seconds, his breath on the back of her neck.

"Tell me I didn't just see a stuffed pink teddy bear in your bag."

"You didn't just see a pink teddy bear in my bag."

Jessica had read about people going weak in the knees and thought it was just an expression—until this man, who seemed to have melted her by the nearness of his body. Her heart thudded so loudly with him this close it blocked her hearing.

He reached over her and flipped the bag open, exposing her teddy bear nestled in her clothing.

Jessica put her hand over the bear, protectively.

"I suppose the bear has a name, like your cat?"

"Esmerelda. My grandmother gave her to me when I was young. She's my good luck charm and always travels with me."

Spencer sighed and returned to the couch. "Get some sleep."

Jessica felt foolish following Spencer's non-reaction. She took her pajamas and went into the bathroom, pulling the door closed behind her. Now she felt doubly awkward at sharing a suite with a man she barely knew.

Jessica dozed off not long after lying down. Once she fell asleep, Spencer's mind started to whir. He played through one potential scenario after another as to how to get her out of this mess with the least damage as possible, but every potentiality was as sticky as the next. He wished he had something hard to drink—like bourbon—but he couldn't find any alcohol in the small, makeshift kitchen. The refrigerator held only some complimentary waters and a bottle of ketchup.

He checked the lock on the door and all the window latches, then peered outside. All quiet. Sitting down on the couch, he leaned back to rest his eyes. It was during this state of half-consciousness that the memory came rushing in.

"Spence! Wake up. Mama wants to dance!"

Spencer's eyes opened. He was nine years old, and it was the middle of the night. He had fallen asleep waiting for his parents to come home.

"Mama, I have school tomorrow. Where's dad?"

"He's asleep. I will write you a note. Let's dance."

His mother's eyes were shiny and excited—as if stars flitted about in them.

Spencer squinted and looked at his bedside clock. Four in the morning. He knew better than to fight this. He sat up, and she laughed and clapped her hands.

"Spence, you simply can't say no to your mother!" She twirled around the room in her purple evening gown. Spencer got dizzy just watching her. He stood up and took her by the arm to steady her. Then they danced together until his mother wore herself out and curled up on his bed and fell asleep. He grabbed a blanket and lay on the floor beside her.

Spencer woke with a start to Jessica standing over him.

He looked up at her, rubbing the sleep from his eyes. Early morning light filled the room.

"I think I can find out if they've identified my fingerprints."

Spencer stretched his neck. "That sounds promising."

"I need a burner phone to set up an untraceable internet hotspot. Then I can gain access to the FBI's and Homeland's servers, to see if there has been anything reported."

"You can do that without being detected?"

Jessica nodded.

"What exactly do you do for Anthony?"

"Forensic auditing. Looking for inconsistencies in company accounting systems."

"How often do you hack into websites?"

"I'm not hacking into government sites—I'm just gaining unauthorized access."

Spencer rubbed the back of his neck. He wished he hadn't fallen asleep sitting up. "How good are you at this?"

"I'm good, okay. Better than good."

"Does it bother you? The hacking?" Spencer had no idea why he was traveling this line of questioning with her.

Jessica's face twisted for a moment. "I hate it. I hate being duplicitous. I've told Anthony that, and he usually only has me hack when it's really necessary."

Was this woman for real? Spencer eyed her, incredulous, thinking of all the women who had come and gone in his life. He felt an odd sense of surprise at the fact that he had never considered the ethics of the women he'd become involved with. Granted, in some instances that would have been a good idea.

Jessica sighed. "I guess I shouldn't really be casting stones. Here I am hacking for my social security number." She paused, eyeing him, her voice softening, "Do you need a neck rub?"

"My neck is fine."

Jessica ignored his response, instead walking around to the back of the couch. She put her hands on his neck and began gently kneading the base of his skull.

"My friend Meg is a massage therapist. She taught me this."

Spencer's first instinct was to reach up and grab her hands and remove them, but he felt a calmness at her featherlike touch. A sense of peace he didn't want to let go of.

"Good, I can feel you relaxing," she said softly.

Her hands felt so warm and certain, and he imagined how they would feel exploring his body. Spencer quickly pulled himself back to reality. "You can stop now," he said, straightening up. He had a job to do, and that didn't include becoming intimate with Jessica. As if he had any chance, anyway.

She removed her hands but remained standing behind him. He could hear her breathing—short, shallow breaths.

"You're welcome," she finally said.

"Thank you, my neck feels a lot better." Spencer stood. "Let me get cleaned up, and then we'll go find a burner phone." What he didn't say was that he planned on one long, very cold shower.

7

Soon after Spencer went into the shower, a sudden rap on the door startled Jessica. She looked from the front door to the shower as the rapping became more insistent, unsure of what to do next.

Opening the door wasn't the answer. She'd have to tell Spencer. She knocked on the bathroom door. No answer. Taking a big breath, she opened the door, the steam hitting her in the face.

Spencer was out of the shower in a flash, quickly pulling a towel around himself. "Something happen?"

"There's someone at the door. I didn't think I should answer it."

"You shouldn't," he said, throwing the towel down and pulling pants out of his bag and slipping them on while Jessica averted her eyes.

"Don't come out until I tell you it's clear, if you want to stay alive. And keep the shower running." Spencer pulled a gun out of his bag.

Jessica did as she was instructed, her heart thudding in her ears. She strained to hear, but the shower masked what was happening in the other room. It seemed like a half an hour, but was probably only five minutes, before Spencer came back in the room, his expression grave.

"It was the hotel owner, and he was fishing. He said he was just checking everything was okay, but he seemed too interested. We need to get out of here right away."

"To where?"

"We'll figure it out. I think we should head out on foot; then find a ride. Pack up."

Spencer left more than enough money for the night's stay in the room. He went to the door and opened it a crack, peering out. Then he opened it all the way and murmured, "Follow me." Locking the door, he slid the key under it. The owner would think they were still inside, and that would buy them some time.

He led them into the jungle terrain next to the hotel. Before long, they were struggling their way through the thick growth, trying not to trip on the tangled vines they met at every step. The thick air buzzed with insects and smelled of damp earth. As they made their way over a fallen log, slippery with moss, Jessica started to slide. Spencer took her arm and gently guided her to solid ground, then took her hand as they continued.

Spencer was batting away at the mosquitos and cursing as they made their way through the jungle.

"I take it tropical climates aren't your favorite." Jessica said.

"Mexico isn't my favorite."

"Did you have a bad vacation here or something?"

"Or something," Spencer said, stopping. He appeared to be accessing their direction. He veered them to the left as bugs continued to fly into their faces and an occasional toad jumped across their path.

"So, you didn't finish about Mexico." Jessica glanced nervously around as they walked, continuing to hang onto him. "What happened here?"

Spencer swung around, causing Jessica to stop short, inches from his face.

"That is not an open subject."

"I didn't realize. I'm sorry."

Spencer kept his gaze fixed on hers, and Jessica willed herself not to look away. The irritation in his eyes softened, and he reached out to gently remove her bag's strap from her shoulder. As his fingers made contact with her arm, a sensation rushed through her chest and belly. Without saying another word, Spencer took her bag and headed them deeper into the jungle.

When they finally spotted a clearing, Spencer slowed his pace. They were overlooking the downtown of the village. Beyond the buildings, fishing boats were docked next to a bay.

"We'll see if we can get a burner phone. If we find a coffee shop with WIFI, would that work?"

"That'd be perfect. I can bounce off their cell towers, and maybe a few more throughout the region."

Whatever it took to get them out of Mexico, he thought. Two days from now, he was supposed to be checking into the lodge in Aspen. A vision of a snowman flashed through his mind, and he flinched.

"Spence, *mi amor*! Your papa is taking us to the snow. *La nieve*. Isn't that wonderful! We can make snowmen all day long—and snow angels, too." His mother had a brochure in her hands and was skipping around the room. Spencer watched his father scrutinize her, the disapproval he had come to recognize turning his blue eyes a dark gray.

"Angelica, please. Why don't you check your closet to make sure you have the appropriate clothing for the snow? I'll have April check the boy's wardrobe."

"Whatever you say, Henry." Then she gave Spencer a big kiss, wrapping him in her arms and swaying to and fro as she giggled. "It will be so much fun, my little love." She kissed both of his cheeks and left the room, the scent of jasmine following her out.

Spencer stood there enjoying the afterglow of his mother's presence when his father barked, "Don't just stand there with your head in the clouds like your mother. Get to your room and start packing."

After a twenty-minute walk out of the jungle and down toward the shore, they arrived at the village. Spencer gestured toward an electronics shop on the corner of the main plaza. When they walked inside, they saw a selection of all manner of electronics, from old television sets to radios and cell phones.

"*Buenos días, Señor,*" said a young man behind the counter when they entered.

"*Buenos días,*" Spencer replied, then asked for a cell phone. "*No mas uno que podemos usar y tirar,*" he added, asking for a disposable phone.

The young man reached under the display case and pulled out a phone. Jessica picked it up and studied its capabilities. She nodded.

That transaction completed, they headed back into the square and spied a coffee shop. Spencer ordered a coffee and was given a WIFI password. They settled into a corner, and Jessica pushed back her blonde hair, a determined look on her face as she started tapping keys on her computer.

After several minutes, she spoke. "It looks like my social has been connected to the name Alexandra Stargazy. I can see a string of expenditures at what looks like a resort outside of Puerto Vallarta. La Jolla de Mismaloya." Jessica turned the computer toward him.

Spencer sat up abruptly, nearly knocking his coffee all over the table. "Stargazy?"

8

"It's an odd name," said Jessica. Do you know it?"

Spencer's family originated from the town where the Stargazy pie was created. Was this a coincidence? Spencer didn't believe in coincidences.

"Is there anything about the person? A record of transactions, maybe?"

Jessica clicked away at the computer, then leaned forward as she read.

"Most likely, it's a woman. There are charges at the spa, a manicure and pedicure, and a lot of bottled water and alcohol purchases. A trip to the hotel's boutique. I need to call this into the Mexican authorities and cut her off. She's racking up thousands under my name."

"You can't, and you know that," said Spencer. "The *federales* would have you then. And you don't want to spend time in a Mexican jail. Any jail, for that matter. We'll find her and stop her ourselves."

"Okay." Jessica tried to put her frustration aside. "What's our next move then?"

"We have to dye your hair."

"What?" Jessica put her hands on her head.

"Something that's going to blend in here a lot better than blonde. You're a walking billboard."

Jessica sighed. "What about a wig?"

"Too traceable. I can go buy you some hair dye."

"Okay, just don't make me a redhead."

Jessica waited in the coffee shop while Spencer went to get the hair dye. When he came back with a white paper bag and set it in front of her, she peeked inside. Chestnut brown. "That works," she said, resigned. She looked around at the half-full coffee shop. "I'll have to do it in the bathroom here, but I'm going to need some time."

Spencer nodded. "I've got an idea."

Spencer waited about ten minutes before approaching the employee on duty. He explained his girlfriend was pregnant and not feeling well and might be in the bathroom for a while. The young man seemed embarrassed by the whole idea and began telling customers that the bathroom was out of service. That worked just fine, thought Spencer as he sat back to wait. He wondered what Jessica's new hair would look like. With her aquiline features, she would be beautiful in any hair color. Then he chided himself. Focus, Spencer, he thought. Figure out how to get Jessica out of this mess.

Jessica eyed herself in the mirror. It was a shock to see herself as a brunette, but it didn't look all that bad. When it dried, it'd be even lighter.

She fluffed it with her hands, then stuffed the empty packaging in her bag and exited the bathroom.

Spencer looked up when she came out of the bathroom—his eyes registering something that he pulled a screen over almost immediately. Just as well, she thought. The sooner she got out of this situation, the sooner she could get back to DC. Although she had to admit, the sound of that didn't hold as much appeal as it did yesterday. Her life in DC was predictable, and, she now realized, a bit dull.

"You look good." Spencer stood, gesturing toward the door. He put a reassuring hand on the small of her back as they made their way out of the coffee shop.

Once outside on the street, Spencer stopped. "When you were dyeing your hair, I found someone to take us to the hotel."

Before long, a battered yellow Nissan Sentra pulled up. The driver jumped out and scrambled over to them. The squat Mexican man announced, "*Señor*, this is your *bonita esposa!* Let us go to your hotel."

Jessica smiled at him in greeting and handed her bag to his outstretched hand. He started to offer to take Spencer's bag but stopped when Spencer stiffened and tucked it under his shoulder.

"*Vámonos, pues,*" said the driver, yanking open the back-passenger door. With a flourish, he slammed the car door behind them and rushed over to the driver's seat, turning the key in the ignition. After a couple of attempts, the car fired to life.

As they drove, the driver looked in the rearview mirror several times before speaking. "How long have you been married?"

Spencer spoke up immediately. "This is our honeymoon. Friends told us that La Jolla de Mismaloya is the best place to celebrate."

"*La luna de miel,*" said the driver, his eyes dancing as he spoke. "I am honored to take you to one of the most *hermoso* hotels in our region. We will be there in about a half an hour." He turned his attention back to the road and cranked up the salsa tunes on his analog car stereo.

Spencer threw his arm around Jessica and pulled her close. She felt her body almost sigh from the impact of his protection. For all his guarded exterior, Spencer had a surprisingly warm and welcoming embrace. Jessica instinctively rested her head against him.

"Spence! Look at the butterflies. *Mariposas hermosas, mi amor.* Do you wish Mama to catch you one that you can take home?"

Spencer nodded vigorously as his mother reached for a large butterfly with blue and green wings in the botanical garden they were visiting.

"Bloody hell, Angelica, stop," his father said, jerking her arm away from the winged creature. "We're not supposed to touch the butterflies—and certainly not take any of them home with us. Get yourself together."

"Of course, we can't take the beautiful butterflies home with us," Angelica said as her face morphed into sadness and tears sprang to her eyes. "I'm so sorry."

Panic and dread set in as Spencer wrapped his arms around her. "It's okay, Mama, I don't need a butterfly," he assured her. The last time something like this happened, he didn't see her sunshiny smile for a long time.

9

When the taxi pulled up in front of the hotel, it was midafternoon. Spencer slid out of the car and reached down for Jessica's hand to help her out. Then he paid the taxi driver. It must have been a good amount of money, because a huge grin covered the man's face. He cried out, "*Buen viaje,*" as they made their way toward the hotel lobby.

"What next?" said Jessica as a valet approached them.

"Checking in, *Señor?*" he asked. "I can take your bags."

"No need, chap," said Spencer, suddenly effecting a British accent.

They made their way into a giant foyer topped with skylights that washed the room in bright sunlight. Palm trees grew out of royal blue concrete planters, and deep green vines spilled over the edge.

When they got to the front desk, a young woman greeted them with a bright smile. "*Bienvenido.* You have a reservation?"

"No, we don't. Hoping you can fit us in?"

She checked the computer. "We do have a suite, *Señor,* on the third floor."

"We'll take it," said Spencer, who pulled out a credit card and handed it to the girl. "She looked at it and said, "*Bueno, Señor* Parker, let me get you checked in."

Once they were standing in front of the elevator, Jessica said in a low voice, "I take it Parker is your alias?"

"One of them." The door to the elevator opened, and he gestured for her to go ahead of him. "Today we're the Parkers, which means we need to get you some identification."

Spencer opened the door to their room, which looked like a small apartment. The room overlooked the pool, and beyond that, the ocean.

"This place is bigger than my apartment in DC," said Jessica, walking to the floor-to-ceiling windows and pushing aside the sheer curtains to look at the pool below.

"Okay, enough sightseeing," Spencer said as he sat down at the dining room table and pulled out the laptop. "Time to fire this thing up and figure out what room our mystery guest is using. You need to triangulate the signal, or whatever it is you people do, so no one can trace your search."

Jessica pulled out a chair and sat down next to Spencer. "So, I'm a 'you people' now? And what happened to your British accent?"

"I use it when I need it."

"Are you British?"

"Yes, half. Go on now." He gestured to the laptop.

"Half British, and the other half?" Jessica questioned as she turned on the burner phone and then powered up the laptop. She would set up a VPN to hide her location, and then her IMSI catcher, so she could pinpoint the Stargazy computer's location.

Spencer started to answer, then stopped himself. What was it about this woman that made him so loose-lipped? Watching her work on the computer, he realized she was easy to talk to. It was her lack of ulterior motives. With most women he worked with and dated there were ulterior motives. But Jessica didn't seem to operate that way. He wondered what her upbringing was like. He smiled to himself as he watched her brow furrow while she typed away on the computer. "What are you doing?" he asked her.

"I set up a VPN to hide my computer's location, and now I'm going to install another device that will allow us to listen to conversations in the hotel."

This intrigued Spencer. "So, we're going to do a stakeout of sorts?"

Jessica smiled at him. "Yes."

"How long is it going to take?"

"It depends on how many guests are here and how many have computers and cell phones." Jessica shifted in her seat.

"You want something to drink?" asked Spencer.

"A soda would be great. Something with caffeine to keep me awake."

Spencer went into the kitchenette and found two sodas in the fridge. No booze, of course. He'd have to buy some. He brought two glasses back to the table where Jessica was tuning into a conversation that could be heard over the computer's speakers.

"There's something I hadn't considered."

"What?" asked Spencer, setting down their sodas.

"There's going to be a lot of conversations in other languages."

"No problem. I speak several."

Jessica looked at him in surprise. "What languages?"

"Spanish, Italian, Tagalong, Russian, and a little Chinese."

"Wow. For your work?"

"It definitely helps."

"Well, what is this couple discussing in Italian, then?"

Spencer listened intently. "He's complaining about how she can't stop thinking about the kids at home and calling them when they're supposed to be having a good time."

They sat there for another two hours, listening to conversation after conversation. Most about mundane things, although occasionally there would be an interesting conversation, like the one now. It sounded like an

American man. "Come back to the room, baby, I've got a giant surprise for you. And it's rock hard." A woman giggled. "I'll be right up."

Spencer laughed as Jessica realized what the conversation was about and quickly switched to another frequency.

"The consequences of eavesdropping," he commented.

Jessica shushed him as they tuned into the next voice. A woman was speaking in Spanish, but there was something about how she spoke that indicated to Spencer it wasn't her native tongue. "You have the number and other documentation, and it's working, so pay up," she said.

"I'll have it for you soon," said another woman, who sounded Latina.

"Now means now."

"We can meet tomorrow. I promise I'll have the rest."

They heard a click, and the woman demanding the payoff muttered something unintelligible and hung up.

"Any way to tell what room she is in?" Spencer asked.

Jessica shook her head. "We have to keep listening to her line until she gives some indication."

It wasn't long before the Latina got on the phone again. After listening to a man's voicemail, she left the message, "*Francisco, mi amor, estoy en La Jolla. Cuarto cuarenta y dos. Ven con champán.*"

"A man is on the way to room forty-two with champagne," said Spencer.

"Let's go." Jessica stood up.

Spencer raised his hand. "First, let's review what we want from her. The woman mentioned documentation. Chances are she has had IDs made, maybe a passport. And there's likely information in her cell phone. She might also have a laptop."

"At what point do I tell her I'm pressing charges?" Jessica put her hands on her hips.

"You're a fugitive in this country, remember? Our goal is to simply retrieve your identification and get out and hope no one else has your information. Then we get back to the US undetected and work out the mess from there."

"Last I checked," Jessica huffed, "nothing is flagging on my name. There's no reason why this woman should escape consequences for what she's done."

"She'll have consequences," Spencer said. "The woman who sold them to her won't take no for an answer."

Jessica studied Spencer's face. "How do you know?"

He opened his mouth to speak, but Jessica's computer beeped. She checked the screen.

"I take that back. I have been flagged. By both the Mexican and American governments."

"Where is that information coming from?" asked Spencer.

Jessica clicked a key on the computer and looked at the results, her heart beginning somersaults in her chest. "Interpol."

10

Any irritation Spencer might have had with Jessica dissolved when he saw the look on her face. "Okay, I'm here to help figure this out. I'll be back in ten minutes."

When he returned, he handed Jessica a maid's outfit.

"You've got to be kidding."

"I know it's cliché, but—." He pulled something from his pocket. "I also have the maid's master keycard."

Jessica shook her head. "I'm not going to ask how you got that."

He grinned. "Probably best."

Jessica took the clothes into the bathroom and shut the door while Spencer sat back. There probably was another way, but this was the most direct route into the room.

Within a couple of minutes, he heard her groan.

"Everything okay?"

Jessica swung the door open and emerged, a grimace on her face. When she stood in front of him in the too-short maid's outfit, which accented her curves, he felt a wave of desire. He stood up and approached her. "You look smashing." He handed her some rubber gloves. He'd already put some on.

Jessica screwed up her face. "You doing the English thing again?" She stood there for a moment looking unsure of what to do, then said, "Let's just get this over with."

Spencer felt oddly deflated, even though he knew she was right. Time was of the essence here.

As Jessica followed Spencer down the hall, she felt an odd sense of excitement. And for a moment, back in the room, she imagined running her hands through his hair and feeling the solidness of his body pressed against hers. Certainly, she was going bonkers out here on the run.

When they reached room forty-two, Spencer whispered to her, "Announce maid service."

"Shouldn't I do that in Spanish? Or at least with a Spanish accent?"

"Give it your best."

Jessica took a second, then yelled out, "Maid service," as she rapped on the door. Spencer checked the hallway, then told her to repeat herself. Still no answer.

He nodded at the doorknob.

Jessica swiped the key and the light turned green. She turned the handle and eased the door open, and Spencer passed in front of her.

"Maid service," she called out again as she followed him into the room, shutting the door behind her. He turned and put his finger to his lips, then took a few more steps inside.

"Dammit all!" he said.

Jessica rushed into the room after him, a small sound escaping her throat. A woman lay on the floor, blood oozing from her forehead.

"Oh, my God!"

"She was shot," said Spencer. "And I don't see any signs of a computer or cell phone. Just this suitcase. He unzipped the case and began poking around, extracting what looked like an address book. Just as he was checking the bureau drawer, someone knocked on the door.

"*Estoy aqui, mi amor,*" a man announced. "*Con champán.*" He knocked again and waited, then it sounded like he left.

Spencer looked out the peephole and held up his finger. After what seemed like an eternity, he eased the door open and glanced outside, then closed the door.

"Keep your head down when we leave the room. I don't think there are cameras in the hallway, but you never know. I'm going to be holding you close, so it'll be more difficult to identify us."

Jessica nodded as he pulled her up against him. The electrical charge she felt every time they got this close seemed to be stronger than ever.

Spencer turned the knob and took another peek out, then pulled her out with him. They walked briskly down the hall and headed toward their room. Just as they were rounding the corner, Jessica's heart slammed into her chest when she and Spencer looked up to see a maid approaching with a cart and a man carrying a champagne bottle. "Into the stairwell." He pushed her and himself through a doorway, which closed just as the maid and man walked past.

"Do you think they saw us?" Jessica whispered, unable to identify any more if her heart was beating or her brain was knocking about inside of her head.

"I don't think so. We need to get to the room and get you out of that outfit." He took her hand and headed up the flight of stairs to their floor. They stopped in front of the stairwell door and Spencer peered out. "Damnit. There's a big group of people coming. Looks like they're going to use the stairs."

Spencer acted quickly by pushing her up against the wall and diving in for a kiss as the door burst open and what sounded like a rowdy bunch of young men came bounding into the stairwell. Loud whistles and catcalls ensued as the group thundered past and headed down the stairs.

Jessica felt startled at Spencer's strong embrace as the kiss that started out as a ruse turning into something fiery and all-consuming. She felt his tongue searching her mouth and her insides melted. The sound of the group of people running down the stairs faded into the distance as her every nerve ending responded to him pressing her against the wall. Spencer moaned and a quiver of desire coursed through her.

Spencer shocked himself at the hunger that overcame him as he tasted Jessica's sweet mouth. The smell of her—soft, a powder-like scent—and sensuous curves pressing against him made him want to tear off her clothes and his and climb into an abyss with her. When he instinctively reached around Jessica's back and slid his hands up inside of the maid outfit's small top, his hands hit the concrete wall and knocked him to his senses. He pulled away. This was crazy! He was being paid to protect her. Breathing heavily, he said, "We need to get back to the room. This isn't safe."

The look in Jessica's eyes was one of both passion and confusion, and she nodded. He eased the door open, relieved to see the coast was clear.

Once back inside their room, Jessica turned to him with a questioning look. Spencer gripped her arms and took up where they had left off in the stairwell, pressing himself against her soft breasts, exploring her neck with his mouth. When her body responded to him and her fingers grasped the back of his hair, he let all logic escape from his brain.

He didn't care any longer what he should or shouldn't do. All he knew was she desired him as much as he wanted her. His mouth kissed along her neck and traveled to the soft cleavage of her breasts as he unbuttoned the front of the maid outfit. Jessica helped him and dropped the straps of her bra as his hot touch traced her exposed breasts. He leaned down to run his tongue over her nipples before devouring her breasts with his mouth. Jessica's body trembled slightly beneath his touch, and she whispered his name in his ear. He pulled her close, not caring at that moment if the earth fell out of its orbit. The tender way she kissed him told Spencer everything.

Suddenly, he envisioned the guilt he would suffer at giving way to his own need. He had never seduced a woman on the job, ever. And he wanted Jessica to believe he was better than that. He forced himself to pull away.

"I'm going out for a minute. I won't be far," he said, turning and stepping out into the hallway. Shutting the door behind himself, he leaned against it. No sound came from the other side of the door, as if Jessica hadn't moved from where he left her. What did she think of him? he wondered. He stood in the hallway trying to keep himself from going back inside. This was a woman he wanted to appear better to than maybe he really was.

11

What on earth was she thinking! Jessica felt horrified the two of them had gotten caught up in the heat of the moment and practically consumed one another. Well, she wasn't going to let the incident torment her and mope around because of it. Spencer was an attractive man—she couldn't deny that. How could she have kept from reacting to his kiss, his touch? If he wasn't interested in her, then so be it. Just then she heard the keycard in the lock. She would pretend like nothing happened and hoped he wouldn't mention it.

Spencer walked in, shifting from one foot to the other as he stood in the center of the room. He had the dead woman's contact book in his hand and cleared his throat. "I've been going through the contact book we got out of the woman's suitcase."

Jessica realized she'd been holding her breath. She tried to relax and sat down in a chair across the room from him, avoiding his eyes. Good, she thought, they could just make out like the entire thing was just a stupid mistake. "Did you find anything?"

"Yes, there are initials R.C. with a California number, and it looks like she met up with the person yesterday. Lucky we found this date book." Spencer flipped through the pages without looking at Jessica.

"Should we contact him?"

"I'm thinking, yes, I should meet up with him. Providing it's a him."

"You mean we should meet up with him," Jessica said.

Spencer opened his mouth as if to speak but shut it again.

"This is my mess," said Jessica. "I appreciate you helping me, but I'm going to be involved until the bitter end. Whatever that end might be." She sat up straighter in her chair. "Give me the number, and I'll check it out."

Spencer handed her the book, the page opened to the number. Jessica entered the number in a database on her laptop as he watched.

"The owner of the number is Rodrigo Cortez. He appears to have had some brushes with the law. Forgery, racketeering."

"Can you track his phone and see where he is right now?"

Jessica hit another screen and entered some information. "Bingo," she said. "Guess where he is right now."

"Mexico?"

"A mile from here."

"I saw a telephone in the hotel's lounge. Let's call him from there and set up a meeting."

"What about when they find that woman's body in the room?" Jessica said.

"I didn't see any cameras in the hallways. I think we're okay for now."

Jessica pushed her chair back and stood. "Do you think my computer and equipment will fit in the room safe?"

"No, and I don't trust room safes. Spencer headed to the corner of the room with a chair. He climbed up and pushed on one of the tiles in the soffit ceiling. "We can hide them up here."

Jessica handed the equipment to him. "I'm going to freshen up, and then I'll be ready. Why don't you go down and make the call?"

Spencer looked down at her and raised his eyebrows at the directive but nodded. "I'll do that."

As he made his way downstairs, Spencer willed himself to think of anything but the feel of Jessica in his arms. The experience left him needy and wanting, and Spencer disdained both emotions.

When he reached the hotel's lounge, he pulled out a prepaid phone card and punched the code into the hotel's courtesy land line, followed by Rodrigo's number.

"*Sí?*" said a hesitant voice after two rings.

"*Señor* Rodrigo?"

There was silence.

"I'm a potential friend in need of information."

"Potential friend, eh?" The man was trying to act cavalier, but Spencer sensed fear.

"If you meet with me and my associate, I can help you get out of Mexico and back to California."

Rodrigo hesitated. "Who sent you?"

"I'm my own free agent."

"*Chinga,*" Rodrigo cussed under his breath. "I'll meet you at the plaza in twenty minutes. I'm wearing a red shirt."

Spencer hung up. Obviously, the man was desperate. Otherwise, he wouldn't have agreed to meet with a stranger in a foreign country. Who was he running from?

In the lobby while Spencer waited for the elevator, a man and woman walked up with a young boy. The man appeared miffed, and the woman held the child close to her.

"All I asked for was a little peace and quiet at dinner, and you couldn't keep him under control."

The woman apologized as they got into the elevator. Spencer entered after them, smiling down at the little boy, whose eyes appeared wide with worry.

"I've had enough of this rubbish!" His father's face was bright red. "The boy didn't go to school all last week. What in God's name is going on,

Angelica?"

Seven-year-old Spencer held his breath as apprehension darted across her eyes. "Spence was sick," she exclaimed. "Don't you remember? I told you he had a sore throat, Henry."

His father scowled, looking from Angelica to Spencer. "Does this have to do with his not liking the English schools? Are you lying to me again, Angelica? Do I need to have one of the staff report the truth to me?"

"No, father, I really was ill. I'll go back tomorrow." Spencer defended his mother.

His father stomped out of the room and slammed the door in their London flat. Minutes later, he heard him leave the building. Spencer turned to his mother, whose eyes were soft with affection for her son. She licked her lips and whispered, "Mama will take you back to Mexico, Spence. Don't tell anyone. It will be our little secret, *mi cielo*. Do you know how much Mama loves you?"

"More than the stars in the sky," he replied.

"Yes, my darling, yes!"

When Spencer got back to the room, Jessica was sipping water and eating nuts from the minibar.

"Did you talk to the man?" she asked.

"Rodrigo is meeting us in twenty minutes in a nearby plaza. I'll be honest, I'm not really comfortable with us being out in the open."

A thread of anxiety snaked through Jessica's belly. "You mean, someone could take a shot at us."

"Precisely."

She glanced at the time on her cell phone. "It's getting late. It'll be dark soon. Maybe that will help?"

Not likely, thought Spencer, but he didn't say anything.

In silence, they walked to the plaza just a few blocks away, stopping near a taco cart falling into shadow as the sun set.

"Did he say how we're supposed to recognize the guy?" she asked.

"Red shirt, but I'll be able to pick him out."

Spencer's eyes scanned the crowd. Children with parents eating popsicles, an older couple admiring the fountain. Teenagers flirting with each other. Then he saw him—a man with a sombrero and red shirt lingering at the edge of the plaza.

Spencer reached out and touched Jessica's arm. "Over there," he nodded. "Stay close to me."

The man saw them approaching and ducked farther into the shadow of a palm tree, his eyes furtive, wary. Spencer and Jessica stopped in front of him, and Spencer said, "Rodrigo. *Tranquilo.* We mean you no harm."

Rodrigo tried to remain blasé, but it was obvious he was spooked. He had a bruise on his cheek, and his arm appeared hurt.

"I don't need any more trouble," he said, reaching into his jeans pocket and extracting a packet of cigarettes. He shook it until one showed its head, then pulled it out with his teeth and lit it. After he inhaled and turned his head to blow out the smoke, he addressed them.

"I'm just looking for *dinero*. You got some good paying work for me, I'm all ears."

"I might. But first, a question. The woman you're supplying with stolen social security numbers. What's her name?"

Rodrigo's eyes widened. "You *loco*?"

Spencer didn't answer.

Rodrigo raised his eyebrows as he blew out another lungful of smoke. "Why you interested?"

"Because she stole my friend's identity, and I need to stop her. My guess is that you made the stolen social security card that led to a murder."

"*Hijole!*" cried Rodrigo. "This wasn't supposed to be complicated." He turned as if to walk away.

"Give me her name, and maybe we can make this all less complicated," said Spencer.

Rodrigo turned back to face Spencer, interest in his eyes. "Just how much less complicated can you make this? How much you offering me?"

"Enough."

Spencer stood his ground. He'd done enough of these types of negotiations to know that when someone was running scared like this guy was, they would eventually cave and give up the information.

Rodrigo took another toke of his cigarette and blew the smoke out. Then he looked at the tip of the cigarette and back up at Spencer and blurted out, "Annika. Annika Morozov."

Spencer thought Rodrigo must be mistaken. "Are you sure?"

"Names are my business."

"Describe her."

"Tall, leggy, blonde, and Russian accent."

"Any other characteristics?"

Rodrigo thought for a moment. "She has a mole on her right cheek."

Spencer met Jessica's eyes, and she asked, "Do you know her?"

12

Jessica studied Spencer's face as Rodrigo told him the woman's name, and Spencer failed to answer about knowing her. She wanted to ask the question again but decided to wait and let it play out.

"So you have some paying work, or is this just a fishing expedition?" A smug expression crossed Rodrigo's face. "If so, I get paid for the fish."

"I do. She needs a passport, pronto." Spencer tilted his head towards Jessica. "And I'll pay you for the fish—providing you give me some bait."

Rodrigo backed up, putting his hands in the air. "Look, I can set her up with a passport, no problem, but that woman is deadly and merciless. She finds out I've led you to her…"

"One passport and the woman's whereabouts, and I'll fund your trip out of Mexico."

Jessica eyed Spencer. Just how much money had Anthony given him to get her out of this jam?

Rodrigo took another long drag on his cigarette. "Let me think about it."

"I wouldn't think too long. The woman you made the social security card for is dead." He took a step closer to the man and looked him in the eyes. "That presents a big problem for you."

"Okay! I'll help you out, but not here. I'll meet you at La Playa restaurant tomorrow morning at eleven. I'll have the passport, but I need her photo to make it."

"I figured that," said Spencer, turning to Jessica.

"Can't we go with him, so I can make sure the photo is deleted?" asked Jessica.

"Rodrigo works alone and clean. I'll erase the photo," he assured them. "Pay me tomorrow morning when we meet. That'll keep me honest."

Spencer raised his eyebrows and nodded. "Go ahead and take her photo."

"But—" Jessica protested.

Spencer turned to her, his jaw tense. "I know this is risky. Believe me. But the passport must look authentic. The only way for him to do that is with your current photo with your new hair color."

Jessica sighed and threw up her hands. "Go ahead." She turned to face Rodrigo.

He snapped a shot of her face with his cellphone. "I can touch it up," he said before scurrying away, soon getting swallowed up by a crowd of people and the evening twilight.

"Are you as hungry as I am?" Jessica asked in the silence following Rodrigo's departure.

"Famished."

Spencer remained on high alert as they found a restaurant and ordered two plates of enchiladas and beans. He struggled to appear unshaken at the news Rodrigo had delivered to them about the woman ordering him to make fake social security cards and documents. Jessica seemed to intuit his knowing Annika, which didn't help. She might be naïve when it came to illegal matters, but she had finely honed instincts. Maybe that's what made her such a stellar hacker, he mused.

"How long have you been hacking for Anthony?" he asked as she scooped up refried beans with a tortilla strip and raised it to her mouth.

She refrained from taking a bite. "What are you talking about? I don't do any hacking, per se."

Spencer laughed.

"What?"

"Are those the exceptions you make when you hack into databases to get information that is vital for the company?"

Jessica looked uncomfortable.

"You can't put a pretty name on it, and it magically becomes something else. Anthony wants you back, because you're his best hacker. I take it you don't get caught."

Jessica sighed, putting the tortilla strip on her plate and leaning back in her chair. "I try not to think about it. And it's not all the time. But yes, it gives me a lot of sleepless nights. Anthony always says it won't happen again, but it does. I've thought about leaving the company, but my parents are so proud that I'm at such a highly regarded accounting firm, and Anthony depends on me."

Spencer noted the worry in Jessica's eyes. "We all have to cross lines at some point in our lives, and they're often not really clear ones," he said quietly.

Jessica looked up from her plate and into his eyes. "How do you live with yourself?"

Spencer was surprised at her straightforward question. He took a long pull on the beer he had ordered, then set the bottle down. Rather than give her a flippant answer, he examined the beer bottle as he spoke. "I suppose I hope the good outweighs the bad."

Jessica nodded slowly.

Spencer finished off his beer. "We should get back to the room. We've been out in the open too long."

A few minutes later, they made their way into the hotel room, and Jessica yawned.

"Go ahead and get ready for bed," he told her.

"What are you going to do?"

"Some strategizing."

Jessica took her bag into the hotel bathroom and looked at herself in the mirror. The darker hair was starting to grow on her.

As she showered, she imagined what it would be like to have Spencer climb in with her. The feeling gave her a rush of excitement that she worked to rinse off with the hot water.

When she emerged a few minutes later, she was surprised to find him asleep on the couch. She watched his level breathing. Where had he come from? What was his childhood like? What were his favorite things to do? He was so tightlipped about everything. She figured she was probably just a job to him—a mission. So there was no need for her to know any of those things. Yet, she longed to have more insight.

She started to head for the bed but stopped and pulled a blanket out of the closet. Gently covering Spencer, she slid into the hotel bed and soon felt herself drifting off to sleep.

"You think I am *estupido*?" Spencer's mother cried, throwing a vase onto the floor in their London flat. "There is another woman. I know it. That's why you're never here with us."

Twelve-year-old Spencer watched as rage flashed across his mother's face. She had spent an entire day cooking a family meal, but his father came late. Her dress was a disheveled mess covered in red sauce and grease. He was pretty sure she'd worn it for the last two days.

"Stop your incessant histrionics, Angelica! You wonder why I'm not here. I can't stand to watch you parade about like a four-year-old, acting younger than our son. If you were an adult, the boy wouldn't be such an insipid milquetoast. You're ruining him. It's time I put him in boarding school, where he can learn to be an adult."

"Don't say such things, Henry. I'll die without Spencer." She ran to his father, hitting on his suit vest.

"Stop it, now!" He ripped her hands from his clothes and pushed her away. She stumbled backwards, threatening to fall on the marble floor, so Spencer ran to try and catch her. *"Está bien, mama,"* he said. "I'll never leave you."

Fury in his eyes, Spencer's father seethed. "You will leave her, Spencer Abbott. Sooner than you expect."

Spencer sat up, looking around the dark hotel room until he regained his bearings. He saw Jessica in the bed, sleeping. Damnit, how he wished he had a drink. To wash down the unwelcome ache in his gut that never fully disappeared at the memory.

Yet another reason to get out of Mexico as soon as possible. Then he'd forget. Like he always did.

But first, he had something to do. It was long past time for a face-off. With Annika.

13

Jessica opened her eyes the next morning to see Spencer gazing out at the ocean view from their hotel room window. What was he thinking about? The more time she spent with the man, the more she wondered about him. She'd had a few relationships in the last couple of years—if you could call them that. More like blips, really. Short-lived and boring. At least that's the way they looked now. Not that this was a relationship, but those guys were so one-dimensional compared to Spencer.

Jessica sat up and pushed her hair out of her eyes. Spencer didn't turn to face her, but said, "How did you sleep?"

"Okay, I think. What about you?"

"I slept for a while." He set down his coffee cup. "Enough."

Jessica slid out of bed and padded over to the table. Spencer yawned as if trying to embrace the morning.

"There's more coffee in the carafe. And I got you a plate of scrambled eggs." He gestured to a covered dish.

"Oh, good." Jessica smiled. She pulled out a chair and reached for the carafe, pouring herself a cup of black coffee and taking a sip. "I've spent many a night auditing and downing coffee. It keeps me alert."

"I would have thought that you took lots of cream and sugar in your coffee."

Jessica laughed. "Why, because of my teddy bear?"

Spencer turned to her. "That and other things."

"What other things?"

Spencer glanced at the time on his cell phone. "We're going to need you alert today. We've got about an hour before we have to leave for the meet with Rodrigo."

"What were you doing when you weren't sleeping?" Jessica asked.

"You asked about my mother's nationality. I was thinking about that."

Jessica was about to take another sip of her coffee but waited. "Yes."

"She was Mexican."

That surprised Jessica. "Oh. Did you spend time here?"

"She was from Veracruz. And, yes, I spent time in Mexico when I was young."

"Is your mother—"

"Still alive? No."

"I'm so sorry. And your father?"

Spencer stood up abruptly. "I'm going to take a shower." He grabbed his bag and went into the bathroom.

It looked like, as usual, she'd asked too many questions. She took a forkful of eggs.

Spencer stripped off his clothing from the day before and stepped into the shower. He had never told anyone in his life about his mother—at all. It was a topic he avoided at all costs, so why did he just blurt that out to Jessica? He lathered up his arms and torso. Because she listened, he realized. And she really wanted to know. Not for reasons that would benefit her. She just wanted to know about him. In an odd way, that comforted Spencer.

"Spence! Mama can't wait to see your piano recital next week. Play a little bit of your song for me right now. *Por favor, mi amor.*"

"But, Mama, I'm not ready yet."

"Oh, Spence, you were born ready. You are an *estrella* already. Play for Mama. Your father isn't here, so you won't anger him. Go ahead."

Spencer sat down at the piano in their London flat and flexed his fingers. His mother sat in a chair facing him, her eyes shining. He began to play a Bach concerto. His fingers ran the length of the piano's keys, returning again and again as he played. When he finished, he looked up to see tears streaming down his mother's cheeks.

"That was magnificent. You made Mama so happy that I'm crying."

Spencer emerged from the shower feeling ready to tackle whatever came their way today. Jessica was wearing a blue dress that accented every inch of her figure. Spencer took in a quick breath. She must have caught something in his reaction, because she asked, "Is this dress okay? It's the only thing I have left that's clean. It's not too conspicuous, is it?"

"It's fine. I was just surprised to see you in something more than your dark pants and shirts."

"So, what should I do when we get there?" Jessica asked for instruction.

"Erase your photo from Rodrigo's phone—permanently."

"That's no problem."

"Other than that just follow my lead."

When Jessica turned to get her purse, Spencer took his gun out and stuck it in the back of his pants, pulling on his jacket.

A few minutes before eleven, they walked into La Playa restaurant. Spencer asked for a table near the entrance, where they sat facing the door. His nerve endings were all standing at attention. If need be, he'd get Jessica out of there in a moment's notice.

He ordered a coffee, and Jessica got an iced tea. "If something happens and we get separated," he told her, "go back to the hotel room and lock yourself inside. Then get in touch with Anthony."

Jessica nodded, her eyes registering apprehension.

It wasn't long before Rodrigo entered the restaurant. He took a quick look around and then trudged toward them with a grim expression on his face.

"You have the passport?"

"*Sí, como no,*" said Rodrigo, sitting down and handing them a brown paper bag.

Spencer looked inside and flipped open the passport; then handed it to Jessica.

"Good work."

"Always," said Rodrigo.

"Would you like a drink? Your work is almost done."

"*Sí.* I could use a beer." Rodrigo rubbed the palms of his hands together.

"Now, about our Russian friend. Where is she?"

Rodrigo pulled a packet of cigarettes from his pocket and lit one, his hand shaking slightly. He shifted in his seat and looked around, motioning for the waiter to hurry with his drink.

"I'm not sure that information is such a good idea." The waiter placed the drink on the table in front of him. Rodrigo waited until the man was out of earshot, lowering his voice. "I think you and your lady friend should get out of here, before someone else gets hurt."

Spencer leaned in closer to Rodrigo. "You don't want to play it this way, Mr. Cortez. I assure you. We are here to get Jessica's social security number back. And we want her photo off your phone."

"I erased it."

Spencer put out his hand. "I want her to check it."

"*Híjole.* Okay." Rodrigo handed over the phone.

While Jessica checked, Spencer reiterated. "Our deal was you were going to give me a location on the Russian. I urge you not to back out now."

"I value my life, *amigo*. And I got another job last night that will give me enough funds to get out of here."

Spencer checked his peripheral vision for anyone else who might be watching.

"Who are you really afraid of?"

Rodrigo's eyes shot open. "The Russian *mujer*. I told you."

"Who is she working with?"

Rodrigo glanced out the window at the street and downed the rest of his beer. "I gotta go. You better, too." He wiped his mouth with the back of his hand. "Give me my money for the passport."

Jessica handed him his phone just as a shot rang out, ricocheting off and blowing the metal napkin holder on their table across the room. Rodrigo bolted from the table as Spencer sprang from his chair, grabbing Jessica. He shoved her through the restaurant door. Once on the sidewalk, they fled into a nearby coffeehouse, running through to the back while customers gaped. They exited out the back door into an alley, where all was clear. From there, they headed to a sidewalk, soon blending into a crowd of tourists filing onto a bus. Spencer wedged himself and Jessica into the line.

As they tucked into a backseat of the bus unnoticed, Spencer cursed to himself. Now they were running from bullets and still had no idea where Annika was.

Before long, the tour leader got on the bus and announced over a loudspeaker inside the bus, "*Bienvenido!* Welcome! We are making our way to Puerto Vallarta's majestic waterfalls today. I hope you brought comfortable walking shoes. Please remember to drink plenty of water. We have a cooler in the front filled with water bottles for you."

"I have some good news," Jessica whispered in his ear once the tour guide paused.

"Let me guess," he replied. "You've always wanted to see the waterfalls of Puerto Vallarta?"

"I got a number off Rodrigo's phone. It looks international. I can probably trace it."

Spencer kissed Jessica on the cheek. When she didn't pull away, he looked at her. Something in his chest tightened, and he had a strong urge to kiss her again. He didn't say anything, but Spencer knew something had changed. Something good. Maybe life and death had a way of doing that, he thought. But it seemed as if a peace had drifted down and settled between them. He didn't quite understand it but was willing to explore this new feeling. First, however, they needed to get to safety, away from gunfire, and then determine where Annika was holed up.

14

When the bus came to a halt in front of a wooded area, the director announced, "Everyone, please exit, and we'll make our way down to an overlook."

As they got off the bus, Spencer leaned down to whisper in Jessica's ear, "Let's stay with the tour for now until we figure out if we've been tailed."

They followed the group to a vista of an expansive canyon filled with deep green vegetation. In the distance, Jessica spied water. The tour guide explained that if you hiked south for just twenty-five minutes, you'd reach a series of magnificent waterfalls.

As they stood waiting with the group, Spencer spied a black car slowing down near the bus. Its windows were tinted. Grabbing Jessica's arm, he guided her to a path heading down towards the waterfalls, and they quickly descended. When they got to the bottom, he stopped under cover of a group of trees and looked up at the tour group. Two suits were searching the crowd. One even pushed a woman aside to peer down toward them.

"Is that the people who were shooting at us?" Jessica whispered.

"Not sure, but they don't look friendly."

"It doesn't seem like they saw us come down here."

"I don't think they did. Otherwise, they'd be after us. But I want to stay here and make sure."

The two men continued to search the crowd for a few more minutes, then one of them got on his cell phone.

"They could be calling in reinforcements to search the area," said Spencer. "Let's head to the waterfalls."

Jessica kept close to Spencer's footsteps, wishing she had on hiking shoes. After walking at a brisk pace for at least twenty minutes, they finally came to a blue pool of water. Spencer sat down on a rock, slapping at a mosquito on the back of his neck. Her mouth like cotton, Jessica reached into her bag and pulled out the bottle of water she had nabbed when they were disembarking from the bus earlier. The bottle was cool to the touch. She took several sips, then handed it to Spencer. "You're a life-saver," he said, taking two long drinks and handing the bottle back to her.

"I was an Indian Princess," she commented as she put the lid back on the water bottle.

"What on earth is an Indian Princess?"

"It's kind of like a Girl Scout, except it's for fathers and daughters. You go camping together and do projects. We even did some mountain climbing together when I was a teenager."

"That sounds like fun. You're close to your father, or were?"

Jessica nodded. "Yes, I'm close with both of my parents. They live in Fairfax, and I see them often."

She slid the bottle into her purse. "I'm guessing you weren't a Boy Scout?"

Spencer laughed. "No, my father definitely wasn't the type. Do you have any siblings?" he asked her.

"No, you?"

"An only child, too." Spencer gazed at the waterfall. "Do you ever think your father wanted a son?"

Spencer's question surprised her. "I've wondered that over the years, but my father has never said anything in particular."

"Is that why you're doing a job you don't like?" Spencer continued his line of questioning. "To please your father?"

"I like my job." Jessica started to protest, but then trailed off. Did she really?

Spencer continued to study her, and Jessica met his intense gaze. He glanced back at the water, then did a quick check of the area. "We seem to be alone. And I think we lost our tail. How about a quick dip?"

"Are you crazy? We can't be sure no one is following us. And I don't even have a bathing suit."

"I'm pretty sure we shook them for now, and I need to get away from these bloody mosquitoes before there's nothing left of me. Wear your undergarments."

Jessica watched in shock as Spencer took off his jacket and shirt, then his shoes and socks. He stuck his gun in some shrubbery next to a boulder and slid out of his pants and underwear, then turned to the embankment and glided right into the water. She observed with a mix of trepidation and envy as he waded up to his chest, then turned around and smiled, daring her to come in with his eyes.

Pushing all thoughts aside for once in her life, Jessica pulled her sundress over her head and gingerly stepped across the moss and into the pool, sighing as the water cooled her hot feet. Spencer was already heading toward the waterfall, and she was thankful he wasn't paying attention. She swam with a languid ease until she came nearer to him. When she was a few feet away from him, she was surprised to find her feet hit sand. Spencer stood under the waterfall, facing away. She watched as the torrent pummeled his strong back, his black hair plastered to his head. Jessica felt almost overcome at the sight of him, remembering his kisses and how his hands caressed every part of her body. At that moment, he turned around and smiled, and it propelled her closer to him.

Spencer watched Jessica approach and thought how she looked so damn sexy with her nipples peeking through her lace bra, brown hair dripping over her shoulders. He couldn't take his eyes off her and struggled against his resolve to take it slow. But when she came to stop and look up at him, Spencer reached out and pulled her lips to his. Had he never kissed before? Spencer's brain was on fire. At last, they pulled away, and he ran his hand along her cheek, the soft skin of her shoulders. He unhooked her bra, tossing it on a nearby rock. Jessica wrapped both arms around his neck then, her soft breasts pressed against his sun warmed skin. No woman had ever made him feel weak in the knees. The effect Jessica had on him made his groin strain hard as his body filled with passion and desire.

He kissed her nose, her cheek, his lips biting gently along her neck and white shoulders, as if he were some kind of primitive being. His hands caressed her nipples and breasts, causing her skin to burn beneath his touch. He leaned his head back, the trees green and lush that sheltered them, the waterfall sprays cooling them, cursing his own weakness. Then he fell to his knees and lowered her panties, the water lapping against him as his mouth sucked and tongue searched that part of her that he wanted only for himself. Her body shuddered as she held him there, fingers tangled in his hair, her cries soft and eager. Then he stood and lifted her leg firmly against him, entering her, again and again, until he could do nothing but hold her tight—so tight that he hoped she'd never want to let go.

15

After they had finished and caught their breaths, Jessica was about to speak when Spencer spied movement in the bushes.

"We've got to get out of the water, now," he whispered, grabbing her bra and pulling her after him as they struggled the short distance to shore. He was out of the water in seconds, reaching under the brush where he had hidden his gun. Still there. He slipped on his clothes and threw Jessica's dress to her. Then he motioned for her to stay close behind him as they made their way toward the shrubbery where he'd seen the movement. When they approached the bushes, Spencer saw a branch move and stopped to raise his gun.

"Don't shoot," he heard Jessica yell when a teenage boy emerged from the bushes, terror in his eyes. Spencer lowered the gun and barked, "What are you doing?"

"I live over there." The young man said, pointing. "I was just going home."

"You were watching us?" Spencer demanded.

The boy vigorously shook his head. "No, *Señor*, I was just passing by."

Jessica reached out her hand and touched Spencer's forearm. "Please put the gun away. You're scaring him."

Spencer stuck the gun in the back of his pants. "You live around here? With your parents?"

The teen nodded. "With *mi papa*. He does tours for *el parque*."

"My wife and I could use a place to stay." He looked at Jessica. "Do you have a room?"

"We have a barn. I would have to ask *mi papa*."

"Is your father here?"

"He is doing a tour right now, but he'll be back soon." The young man hesitated, looking at Jessica.

"Would it be okay if we went to your *casita* and waited for your father?" she asked him gently. "We mean no harm."

The teen appeared uncertain at first.

"I am Joslyn, and he is Mark. What is your name?"

"It is Cortez, *Señora*. Like the explorer. That is my first name. My surname is Castellano Hernandez."

"What a nice name." Jessica gave the boy one of her melt-your-heart smiles, and Cortez's eyes became less doubtful. He finally announced, "I will lead you to our *casita*."

They followed him up an embankment that soon led to a clearing and a small adobe house. Next to it was a small barn made of salvaged wood.

"What do you keep in the barn?" Jessica asked.

"The milking cows and sheep when they're not grazing. They are in the pasture now." He turned and motioned for them to follow him into the house.

The little home had one good-sized room with a crude kitchen area and what looked like a combined family room and dining area. A door at the back of the building appeared to lead to sleeping quarters.

"You are welcome to wait for *mi padre* here." Cortez gestured to a horsehair couch at one end of the room that sat near a potbellied stove.

After about thirty minutes, the boy's father approached the house. Cortez jumped up, then ran outside to greet him. After some conversation, the older gentleman entered the home, questions in his eyes.

"I am *Señor* Heriberto Hernandez," he announced. "How may I help you? My son says you are looking for a place to sleep. There are hotels a few miles away that I can take you to."

Spencer stood up and approached Heriberto, his hand outstretched. "Nice to meet you. My wife and I are looking for an authentic experience here in Mexico. We'd like to stay in the barn, if that's okay with you. I can pay you well for the privilege." Spencer reached into his pocket and pulled out a wad of money.

"I have heard of such vacations. We have never had anyone here before, however. I'm afraid our accommodations are quite crude."

"The more rustic, the better." Spencer announced, handing him several hundred. The two men shook hands, and before long, they were chatting about Heriberto's work as a tour guide.

After a time, Spencer said, "Well, we better get out of the way. We don't want to disturb your wife when she comes home." At that, Heriberto's smile faded. "My wife is no longer with us. She died several years ago."

"That is very sad to hear," said Jessica.

Heriberto looked at her shyly and said, "*Gracias, Señora.*"

"Let's go to the barn, dear," said Spencer, "and let them have their dinner."

"Oh, but you must stay with us for the meal," said Heriberto. "Cortez," he called out to the boy, who sat in a corner of the room. "Go to the stream and catch some fish for dinner, and we will have the squash you grew in the garden, and some frijoles and tortillas."

Cortez responded immediately by grabbing a fishing rod off a peg on the wall and heading out of the *casita*.

"That's very kind of you," said Spencer. "Okay with you if we check out your barn?"

"*Sí, Sí,*" said Heriberto. "Sleep in the hay loft. Sometimes one of the animals will wander back to the barn in the night."

16

Jessica watched Spencer eye the hayloft and repressed the urge to laugh. She had a feeling he'd never been camping in his life. Her eyes followed the ladder up to the loft as thoughts of their time in the waterfall filled her head.

Climbing the rungs made of twine, she pulled herself up, then landed on a mound of hay that prickled through her clothing. There were bales piled to the left and right, but it looked like there would be enough room to sleep.

"How is it up there?" Spencer asked.

"It's something."

"Hopefully, we'll soon be out of here."

"Any idea how we'll do that?" Jessica called out as she descended the ladder. Silence from Spencer. When she got to the floor, she saw him standing stock still eyeing a snake several yards away.

"Stay there. Don't bat an eyelash. I'll help you," she said in a low voice.

Spencer seemed frozen to his spot. "I'll take any help I can get."

Her breath catching in her throat, Jessica scanned the area for a weapon, and her eye fell on an axe hanging on a wooden beam nearby. She took several steps backward and lifted the axe from its perch. The movement caused the snake to move, and Spencer cussed, "For shit's sake."

Bringing her arm back with force, Jessica aimed at the snake and threw the axe forward. It landed with a hard thud, slicing the snake in half.

Spencer turned to her, the shock in his eyes almost making her giggle. "Where did you learn that skill?" His muscles relaxed.

"Javelin tossing. I was the school champion." Jessica went over and examined the snake, which had stopped convulsing. She turned to face Spencer; shock still registered in his eyes.

"Thank you," he said quietly.

Something clutched in Jessica's heart at the genuineness of the statement. "You're welcome."

An awkward silence ensued, and Spencer finally broke it. "Okay, well, we have to figure out our next move."

"If I can get access to WIFI, I can trace that international number."

"I have a feeling our hosts can't help us with that. Maybe they know someone in the area who can. Let's go see what's for dinner. Hopefully, not snake."

Jessica laughed as they headed for the barn door. The late afternoon light peeking in around the edges of the door was bright, so she instinctively closed her eyes as Spencer pushed the door open.

When she opened her eyes, the lush vegetation of the jungle greeted her. "It sure is beautiful here," she remarked at the vista from the barn. Walking through the land cleared around Heriberto's home, she stopped at the edge of a ravine. Spencer came to stand beside her.

Spencer had to admit this was a breathtaking sight. He fought the urge to take Jessica's hand as they marveled at the view together. Turning to watch her profile, he noted how content she looked. Like she belonged to this simpler way of life. Hacking for Anthony seemed to be eating away at her. He wondered if he should talk to Anthony about that, but no, that wasn't his business.

They watched the sun dip below the jungle, causing the ravine to slip into darkness. Then they turned and went back to the house, where the door stood open.

"*Vente,*" called out Heriberto. "Cortez caught us a giant marlin."

"It smells heavenly," said Jessica, who walked across the floor to see the fish cooking over a camp stove in the tiny kitchen. The smoke coming from the stove was filtered through a bamboo pipe that headed out through the rough ceiling.

"*Cerveza?*" Heriberto held a beer out to Spencer, who gladly took it.

Their host motioned for Spencer to sit down on the horsehair couch as he perched on top of a stool. Spencer heard Jessica speaking with Cortez over by the stove, her gentle voice tinged with real interest in the boy, who had brightened up and was sharing about his studies.

"She is a woman of strength and beauty, and very intelligent," said Heriberto, who glanced over at Jessica as she leaned in to take a good look at the marlin cooking. "You are a lucky man. I do miss my Sarabella. But you don't wish to talk of sadness."

Spencer shifted on the chair, tearing his eyes away from Jessica and focusing on Heriberto.

"We appreciate your hospitality and do wish to ask if you could help us further."

"Anything," said Heriberto.

"My wife is concerned for her mother's health. If there is any way she can get to internet access, so that she can contact her, I know it would ease her mind. We don't wish to leave our trip—just check in." Spencer figured it was a long shot, but it didn't hurt to throw the request out there.

"*Cómo no.* There is an *Americano,* who lives a half mile north of here. He has a satellite system and internet. I know him well. His name is Tony. We can go there tomorrow morning, if you like."

"That would be wonderful," said Spencer. "What does he do, this Tony?"

"He is a writer."

Spencer wasn't thrilled about needing help from an unknown writer holed up in the middle of the Mexican jungle. But he had what they needed, desperately. Internet access. As far as Spencer could see, they had no other choice.

17

They spent the evening eating the fresh fish and squash from the garden and chatting about life in the jungle. Heriberto amused them with stories about his experiences as a tour guide.

"One *hombre*—I think he was from Germany—had too much *cerveza* and passed out on the tour bus. I couldn't wake him up."

"What did you do?" asked Jessica.

"I waited until he sobered up. It took hours. Not until the sun was about to come up did he sit up, and then he just walked away."

"Cortez tells me he wishes to also be a tour guide," said Jessica. The young boy cast her a shy smile.

Heriberto sat up, pride filling his chest. "*Sí*, but I told him he must finish his studies. Us tour guides must have the knowledge and language skills to tell people about this area. About what to expect when they are hiking, but also about our ancestors. We have a rich history here."

"I am seeing that," said Jessica.

Spencer noted that Heriberto, though still a lively host, was beginning to tire.

"Well, we won't keep you," he said. "*Muchas gracias* for a wonderful meal and good conversation."

"*Sí, Señor* Parker. We don't have many visitors here, so it is our pleasure." He stood to shake Spencer's hand. "I only work a short time in the early morning tomorrow. I can take you to *Señor* Tony's after I get back."

Jessica said her goodbyes, then they headed out of the casita. As they did so, Spencer reached out and took her hand. She looked at him, surprised at the tender gesture. "For show," he mouthed, though truth be told, he wanted to hold her hand.

Before they climbed the ladder back at the barn, he grabbed his jacket. As they settled in the loft, he handed it to her. "Use it for a pillow, if you want."

"What about you?"

"I'll get the full camping effect without it."

Jessica rolled up his jacket and laid her head to rest on it. "I can't believe how sleepy I am," she murmured.

Spencer lay down near her on his back and smiled when he heard her breathing soon slow. Though he was exhausted, he remained awake listening to mice scurry about in the rafters and an owl hoot outside.

"Spencey! It's Mama. Wake up."

It was the middle of the night. They were at a cabin in the Swiss Alps.

Spencer sat up in bed. His mother wore her pajamas—her long black hair hanging free, spilling down her back.

"Come! Your father won't know." Spencer recognized the look on his mother's face. Her eyes were feverish.

"Where, Mama?"

"Some last fun before we drop you off in that boring boarding school tomorrow. Come!" She tugged on his arms, and he knew there was no changing her mind.

"Where is father?" Spencer swung his legs over the edge of the mattress.

"He's gone out on one of his secret dates with that horrible woman. He thinks I don't know. But I do."

Spencer's gut clenched. He'd seen the woman once when she came to the house and his mother had been sedated by the doctor. His fists clenched. How could his father betray them like that?

"Come, Spencer." His mother's eyes danced. "The maid is sound asleep. I made sure of it."

"What did you do to the maid, Mama?"

"I gave her some of your father's whiskey. She really liked it." She laughed. "Now put on your snowsuit. The moon is full."

Spencer jerked awake. It only took him a second to reorient and bring himself back to the now, but the pain from the memory seared his chest. He quickly wiped away a stray tear at the corner of his eye. Jessica shifted in her sleep and turned toward him, slipping her arm across his chest. At the feel of her soft flesh against his, the pain in his chest soon eased. He reached around with his free hand and stroked her soft hair as he felt himself drifting off to sleep.

A bright, hot sun casting light fractures across the hayloft from fine cracks in the wooden ceiling woke Spencer the next morning. He sat up and looked around, then called out, "Jessica?"

Silence.

He climbed down the ladder to discover that she was nowhere in the barn, but the door stood open. Stepping out into the sunshine, he wondered about the time. Then he heard her unmistakable laughter coming from Heriberto's house. Peering through the doorway, he saw Jessica with a fishing net on her lap and a needle in her hand. She looked up, mirth in her eyes.

"I'm sewing Cortez's net. Last night's marlin created a huge hole. See?" She lifted it up as Spencer approached.

"She is doing a good job," said Cortez, who was working on a wood carving. He set down the piece and stood. "Would you like some breakfast, *Señor*? *Mi papa* will be back soon."

"Some coffee would be great. And whatever you both ate."

"*Huevos con frijol?*"

Spencer nodded. "*Gracias.*" He sat down next to Jessica and watched as she expertly stitched the large hole, bringing the netting together in a tight tapestry.

"Something else you learned as an Indian Princess?"

"No, from my mother. She's an excellent seamstress." Jessica stopped stitching and eyed him. "You look like you got some good sleep."

"I did. You?"

"I didn't know that hay could be so comfortable. Though I have to say a bath would be wonderful."

Spencer's mind flashed to the waterfall, and Jessica's must have, too, because she reddened and began to stitch in earnest again.

"When Heriberto returns, we'll go see the American."

Jessica nodded, tying a knot in the thread and then separating the thread from the net with her teeth. She held up her handiwork and announced, "Good as new."

Cortez approached with a plate piled high with eggs and beans and a mug of coffee. "*Bueno, Señora* Jessica. "Now I can catch even bigger fish, and none will escape."

Not long after, Heriberto arrived. "I am done with my work for the day. We can head over to *Señor* Tony's whenever you are ready."

"How about now?" Spencer suggested. "We're quite anxious to get through to Jessica's mother."

Jessica's raised her eyebrows, but answered smoothly, "Yes, the sooner I call her, the better."

"Of course," announced Heriberto. "*Las Madres* worry, and we wouldn't want that."

Spencer and Jessica followed Heriberto out of the casita. "The trail is clear for most of the way. But watch out for snakes."

As they headed toward the unknown, Spencer checked the position of his gun, hidden under his jacket. Hopefully he wouldn't have to use it today.

18

Heriberto led them through the brush to the American's house. As he slashed their path open with a machete, he gave a running dialogue about the Sierra Madre through which they traveled.

Soon after, they came upon a small cottage. The front door suddenly swung open, banging against the side of the house. A tall, muscular man waited with his arms crossed as they made their way toward him.

"*Señor* Tony," Heriberto exclaimed as they headed toward his neighbor. "I will speak with him first." He instructed Jessica and Spencer to wait.

The man appeared to be in his early fifties. His stance said that he had every intention of protecting his homestead and way of life. He and Heriberto spoke briefly in Spanish as Tony periodically glanced back at them—mainly at Spencer. Finally, they waved for them to approach.

"Heriberto tells me you two are experiencing the Mexican countryside," said Tony. "Mrs. Parker, you need to use my WIFI satellite service to contact your mother? And Mr. Parker, I understand you're a travel buff?"

"Yes, it would be lovely if I could use your computer to contact my mother," said Jessica.

"My good buddy Heriberto says that you're willing to pay for the privilege of using my internet?"

Spencer leveled his gaze at Tony and nodded. "That's right."

Tony studied him, his eyes flicking to Jessica and back again. They must have passed some sort of test, because Tony unfolded his arms and said to Heriberto, "That should work out."

Heriberto smiled. "*Gracias, Señor* Tony. I'll leave you all, if that's okay?"

"That's just fine," said Tony. "Good seeing you."

After their host headed away, Tony opened the door to his house and gestured for them to enter.

The house was solidly built, and unlike Heriberto's home, had many modern conveniences, including a fully equipped kitchen. A skylight cast bright light onto what looked to be Tony's office, complete with a computer, printers, and telescope.

"This whole place runs on solar power," Tony said. "I've got a bunch of batteries out back that fuel up with the sun. My water comes from an aquifer."

"This is lovely," said Jessica.

"Go ahead and make yourselves comfortable," said Tony. Jessica and Spencer took seats, while Tony pulled up a chair to face them.

"Okay, let's cut the crap. I'm former California PD, and I know you're up to something. How long have you been in Mexico, and why are you here?"

Jessica opened her mouth to speak but Spencer got there first.

"That's two questions, but I'll answer. We've been in Mexico about three days. We're here because her social security number was compromised. We need to stop the woman who stole it."

The man nodded, seemingly satisfied with Spencer's forthrightness. "What agency are you with? I can see you're carrying."

Spencer decided to keep going if they were going to trust each other. Because right now they needed this man's trust—and help.

"Secret Service consultant, and other odd jobs to keep me flush. My real name is Spencer Abbott."

"I have buddies at the Secret Service and the FBI," said Tony warily. "I can easily check you out."

"We'll wait right here," Spencer replied.

Tony went to his office and picked up a phone. After speaking a few minutes in a low voice, he hung up and returned to sit with them.

"I see you're legit. And I'm guessing you didn't give me her real name for a reason?"

"How about we hear why you're really here," said Spencer.

"A journalist buddy got me down here—Jesse McMillan. He's big time —won a bunch of awards for his investigative pieces. He asked me for some help on an investigative series he's doing. My personal life had just taken a nosedive, so I agreed."

"Are those articles classified?" Spencer asked.

"I can tell you this. They involve various foreign nationals who've made Mexico their playground. The list includes one Russian foreign operative the buddy I just called tells me you're likely down here tracking. Annika Morozov. I understand you know her well?"

Until now, Jessica had been quiet, but Tony's words stunned her.

"Spencer. You know Annika? What is going on?" She stood up, unsure of what to do with herself. This news was as shocking as it was maddening. From the moment she'd met this man, he'd been withholding things from her—about her. It reminded her of how Anthony treated her. All the need-to-know nonsense.

"Sit down, Jessica."

Jessica stayed standing. "Explain this all to me, right now. Or maybe, he can," she said, looking directly at Tony.

Tony raised his eyebrows. He turned to Spencer. "You want to tell her who Annika is to you?"

"I will. In the meantime, let me pay you for the use of your WIFI."

"Fair enough. Three-hundred dollars will do. I'll be working out back."

Spencer pulled three one-hundred-dollar bills from his wallet and handed them to Tony, who got up and put the money in a safe beneath his desk. "The password is underwater scrolls—555. I'll be outside for awhile."

Once Tony was out of earshot, Jessica said, "Either you tell me who Annika is to you, or I don't hack into anything."

Spencer sighed. "Annika is—was—my stepmother."

19

Jessica was incredulous. "You forgot this vital piece of information?"

"Obviously, I didn't forget," Spencer said dryly.

She began pacing in front of the couch. "I have never met someone as exasperating as you," she finally exclaimed, stopping in front of him. "How is this coincidence even possible?"

"I knew something was off when we ran into the name Stargazy. That was a code word my father and Annika had between themselves."

Jessica sat back down, waiting for Spencer to continue. They sat in silence for a time, the only sound the slight hum of Tony's computer equipment.

"Oh, hell," he said, finally. "Annika was never a mother in any sense of the word. Step or otherwise. She is a lethal Russian operative, who makes her spending money running identity theft and counterfeit scams. She hooked up with my father years ago. He came from an old family—of some nobility. But truth be told, the family money was limited, then nonexistent when he frittered it away gambling, so he got sucked into her scams."

Spencer stopped and took a breath.

"My father was well-connected. He knew diplomats and foreign dignitaries. His affair with Annika ended up being a Bonnie and Clyde story that ended with him dead."

"Oh, Spencer," Jessica said, softening. "I'm so sorry."

"Don't be," he said bitterly. "He was never much of a parent."

Spencer rubbed his palms over his face. "After my father left my mother for Annika, he made many bad decisions, some including my mother." He stopped. "I've talked enough. Let's work on identifying Annika's whereabouts now."

Jessica wanted to understand more, but she willed herself to focus on the task at hand. She took out her burner phone, logging into the WIFI using Tony's password. "Then she entered the number she'd gotten off Rodrigo's phone. Within a few minutes, she announced, "I have the coordinates. Let's see where she's located now."

When the location came up, Jessica's heart jumped into her throat. "She's near my house. In DC. Oh, my God, Meg!" Jessica looked up at Spencer. "What should I do?"

"Call your friend. Make sure she doesn't go to your apartment. At all. Put her on speaker phone."

With shaking fingers, Jessica dialed Meg's cell phone, praying that she picked up. Finally, she heard a tentative hello.

"Meg, it's me, Jessica."

"What is going on? I went to your apartment to feed Natalia a little while ago, and there was a Russian woman there, petting her."

Jessica gasped. "What happened?"

"She said she was a business associate and just stopping by. That the door was unlocked. That's when I knew she was lying. I told her to leave, and she got this creepy smile on her face. She put Natalia down, and said to tell you hello. I talked to your super after she left. He's going to change your locks. I took Natalia and got out of there."

"Thank you for getting Natalia, and I'm so sorry. If you see that woman again, call the police."

"Don't call the police," Spencer interrupted. "Let me give you a number to call."

"Who's that?" asked Meg.

"Spencer. He's assisting me with things."

"Things? Jess, I'm worried about you. Are you okay?"

"Give Natalia love for me, Meg, and stay away from my place."

Spencer dictated the number for one of his Secret Service buddies.

When Jessica hung up, she commented, "How are we ever going to catch up with Annika now that she's in DC?"

"She went to your apartment to make a statement. She's most likely on her way back to Mexico right now."

"How do you know?"

"I know how she thinks. In the meantime, we wait."

Jessica watched Spencer closely. Though he sounded matter of fact, and his eyes were determined, he appeared more on edge than she had seen him during this whole misadventure.

"Spencey, look what Mama bought you! A beautiful bracelet made of black onyx. This is for good luck, *mi amor*, and to always protect you. It will help you with your studies." She slid it on his wrist, then hugged him hard.

"I don't want to go to boarding school," he whispered into her black hair that smelled of sunshine. "Can't I stay home? Someone needs to take care of you."

His mother stopped hugging and looked into his eyes. *"Mi amor,* you are thirteen now. It is time for you to get schooling, so that you can get a good job and have your own family one day. Mama will be fine. And I will see you at Christmas, *recuerdas*? We will have so much fun making snow angels. And we will stuff ourselves with candy canes."

Spencer gazed into his mother's eyes, searching for the signs. Had she been taking her medicine?

"Time to let the boy go," said his father as he and his mother parted.

"I'm fine, *hijo. Cierto.*" Tears glistened in his mother's eyes. She pointed to the dining hall where the new students were congregating for an assembly. "Go now. Make friends."

Spencer smiled at his mother before turning to file into the cafeteria. He would never know the answer to his question, because that was the last time he ever saw her.

20

"What now?" asked Jessica. "What do we do with ourselves while we wait for Annika to come back to Mexico?"

Spencer gave her an intense smile. "We could go take another dip by the waterfall." A wave of desire went through her at the thought, but she changed the subject.

"Shouldn't we be checking in with Anthony? Let him know what's happening with my social security number?"

"That's probably a good idea," said Spencer. "I'll call from your burner." She watched as he dialed her boss's number, pushing visions of the waterfall encounter out of her head.

"Straight to voicemail."

"That's odd," she said, snapping out of it. "Anthony usually jumps on his phone calls."

Tony came in the back door then. "How's it going? You get through?" He walked into the kitchen and opened the refrigerator.

"Yes, thanks for the use of your equipment," said Spencer. "Hoping we can check back in tomorrow?"

"Yeah, sure, go ahead. I actually felt kind of bad about the money I charged you when I was out back chopping wood. No need to pay me any more cash tomorrow."

"We'll get out of your way." Spencer stood up and Jessica followed suit.

"Feel free to hang out, if you want. To be perfectly honest, I start to go a little stir crazy out here all by myself. I'm not much of a cook, but I make killer eggs and fried potatoes, if you want a late lunch."

Spencer looked at Jessica and raised his eyebrows.

"That would be wonderful," she said.

They spent the rest of the afternoon and evening enjoying Tony's colorful tales about his time as a police officer and narcotics agent. On several occasions, Jessica laughed so hard, she thought she might burst. Tony also told them about life in the jungle. How challenging it was to get his house built like he wanted—even with his construction background. And how it took a lot of trial and error with the batteries to get it just right, so he had electricity. He also grew some of his own fruits and vegetables.

They ate fresh papayas with their eggs and potatoes, and Tony told them how he fertilized the trees with eggshells.

"This is delicious," said Jessica as she relished the sweet and savory combination.

"When I came here, Heriberto taught me how to live off the land." Tony patted his washboard stomach. "The lean, good eating is keeping me healthy. I had no idea how to cook when I got here. Heriberto gave me some of his wife's recipes, especially how to use the fruits and vegetables, and after a bunch of experimenting, I finally made something edible."

On several occasions, Jessica caught Spencer studying her as they all talked, and he gave her a warm smile.

When night began to fall, they sat outside in the twilight to watch the sky and wait for shooting stars. Tony said he saw one at least once a night at this time of year during the dry season. Sure enough, Jessica spotted one and tried to quickly make a wish, but she couldn't decide which she wanted more. To get home and back to her life or to stay here with Spencer.

When the conversation quieted later in the night, Tony walked them back to the barn, a flashlight leading the way. After saying goodbye, they went in and climbed up into the hayloft, laying down next to each other, inches apart.

Jessica awoke with a start. Spencer was talking in his sleep. He cried out Mama several times and begged his father about something. When his arm lashed out and could have struck her, she caught it, and he opened his eyes, confused.

"Bad dream," she said. "You're okay. We're okay."

Spencer looked toward her in the dark and then pulled her face to his and kissed her. Jessica realized at that moment that she was falling harder than she ever had. As if he could read her mind, he kissed her again, long and deep. She pressed her face into his neck, loving the scent of him. "Hold me close," she said, and wondered how he felt about her, but couldn't ask. The thought of being without him gave her a twinge of anguish.

Thin rays of moonlight came through the chinks in the wall and fell on the bales of hay. "If I could give you the moon, I would," Spencer said, reaching a hand into the rays as if he could capture them for her in his fist. His words made her happy, and he felt strong and warm against her. Then he said something that made her breath stop flowing and took the words from her mouth. "Could you love me, Jessica?"

"Why are you asking me that?" she finally said as the words hung in the air. He leaned up on one arm, and she looked at the outline of his face in the dim light. "Because I think I'm in love for the first time in my life," he said quietly.

So much joy coursed through Jessica, it felt as if she were someone she didn't know. And still she said nothing. Instead, she put her palm on his chest and let her hand drift across the smooth skin of his stomach to his erect penis. Then she began to caress him. When he grew stronger, she straddled him, guiding him inside her, slowly moving until he took hold of her hips, moving with her, up and down, up and down. Her hair fell against his chest in the dark.

When she felt Spencer try to stop his urgency and pull from her, she became insistent and held him there, until at last a rapturous, violent spasm shook them both. Jessica collapsed softly on his chest. She panted for a moment, wanting to give him an answer, her heart filled with tenderness. Then she said, "I think I loved you from the beginning."

21

When Jessica awoke in the early morning hours with her head still nestled on Spencer's chest, she thought he was still asleep, until he spoke.

"You wanted to know about my mother," he said, his voice just above a whisper. Jessica lifted her head slowly, until her eyes met his.

"Only if you want to tell me."

"I've never talked about her. With anyone. But I want to tell you."

Jessica reached out and rested her hand on his chest. She felt his heart beating, slow and steady.

"I called her Mama, and we were best friends. I spent most of my time with her. My father had business obligations, so we traveled back and forth from Mexico to England. I often had tutors and became rather shy as a result. That bothered my father. He was always putting me into schools, and my mother would make excuses to keep me home."

"Sounds like she loved you very much," Jessica murmured.

"In many ways, my mother was a child. I didn't know it at the time, but she suffered from a severe case of bipolar disorder. It wasn't diagnosed until I was ten. The medication for the disorder wasn't good for her. It dulled her down. She hated taking it and would often pretend to. Then she'd have episodes of mania. My father became increasingly frustrated with her, even though he was mesmerized by her. Over time, her wide mood swings wore him down. He responded by becoming angry and distant, and then..."

"Other women?"

"Yes. But my mother knew. And it ate her up inside." Spencer started running his fingers through his hair. His brow furrowed as he continued. "One night before my father packed me off to boarding school, I heard her screaming about some Russian woman. I know now that it was Annika. Mama became so incensed; he had a psychiatrist come and sedate her. It took her a week to come back to herself. By then, it was time to take me to boarding school in Switzerland. Mama came along to drop me off."

Spencer stopped talking then. His heart had sped up.

"That must have been so difficult for you to leave her," said Jessica.

"The night before, I had my last outing with her. We were staying at a hotel near the boarding school, and Father had left the hotel room. Mama woke me in the middle of the night, excited. It was snowing outside, and she wanted us to go out and experience it. There wasn't ever any snow in Mexico."

"That sounds like such fun," said Jessica, rubbing her hand across his chest.

"It was fun, even though I was older at the time and self-conscious about other students possibly seeing me. But my mother had such a way about her that she could talk me—and others—into just about anything." Spencer stopped and swallowed.

"We ran around in the snow at first, tipping our faces to the sky and sticking our tongues out. Then we made snow angels. We were lying in the snow, laughing as we moved our hands and legs, just as my father walked up and yelled, 'Bloody hell, Angelica!' He had Annika with him, and that set my mother into a frenzy, especially when Annika commented that my father should have my mother committed. He eventually managed to get my mother back into the hotel room and calmed down, and I was ordered to bed. The next day when they dropped me off at school was the last time I saw my mother."

After an extended silence, Jessica asked, "What happened to your mother?"

"Father took Annika's advice and committed her to a hospital for the mentally ill in Mexico. When I came home for the holidays from boarding school, he told me she had died. Suicide. There wasn't even a funeral."

"Oh, Spencer," Jessica said as she watched his usually strong face crumple into pain. "I'm so, so sorry."

"Soon after, Annika entered my life. Fortunately, I spent most of my time at boarding school. Let's just say that we never got along."

After Spencer had finished, he said. "There you have it. The story of my main influence." He waited, wondering how she would reply.

Jessica put her hand on his cheek and simply said, "It sounds like your mother loved you the only way she knew how."

This woman. How she said things so simply. She was right. He pictured his mother back then twirling in her dresses, giggling like a schoolgirl, taking his hand. Telling him she loved him—to the moon and back again.

Just then, Heriberto called from outside of the barn, "*Señor y Señora! Señor* Tony wants to speak with you. He says it's urgent!"

"Looks like memory lane will have to wait," said Spencer, sitting up quickly and swinging around to climb down the ladder with Jessica following.

When they pushed open the barn door, Tony was standing there. He looked agitated.

"So, I check the wire every morning, you know for any scuttlebutt I need to know about. The Mexican *federales* are looking for a woman they're calling a master hacker, who is wanted in connection with two deaths of Mexican citizens. She was last seen with a man fitting your description. They're concentrating on this area right now. We gotta get you guys out of here, pronto."

"I'm so sorry," Jessica said.

"Look, I don't think for a minute you whacked anyone. But here, it's guilty until proven innocent. Also, that cell phone you were tracking. I'm guessing that it's Annika's. One of my sources told me she's at a hotel by the coast, La Jolla de Mismaloya."

"That's where our room is," remarked Jessica.

"That's where we're going now," said Spencer. He started to pull cash out of his wallet, but Tony stopped him. "How about you pay the guy I'm going to have get you out of here? There will probably be roadblocks going up, so we're going to improvise. Hope you like papayas," he added.

A few minutes later, a truck pulled up with a flatbed trailer in tow. The back had a four-foot-high bed filled with a three-foot mound of papayas. The driver hopped out and walked around to greet them.

He wore a straw hat and had a steady hand as he shook theirs.

"*Mucho gusto*," he said to Spencer in greeting, his handshake firm. "*Me llamo* Juan." Then he turned to Tony, and they hugged and slapped one another on the backs.

Spencer withdrew a wad of one-hundred-dollar bills and handed them to the man, who nodded in thanks.

"He doesn't speak any English," said Tony. "I already explained how you need to get into Puerto Vallarta under the radar. But if you get caught, Juan had nothing to do with this. You jumped on at one of his stops. Good luck, man. Check in with me when this is all over and we can get together and tell war stories."

22

The truck bounced in and out of potholes, which sent the fruit rolling around them. After about an hour, when Jessica had begun to relax and think they might successfully slip into the city unnoticed, the truck slowed. She watched as Spencer spied over the back of the bed into the truck cab, then swore and lowered himself, saying in a low tone, "Roadblock."

Jessica hunched down, covering herself with as much fruit as she could, while Spencer presumably did the same. Juan slowed the truck to a near crawl, most likely to ensure that the fruit stayed on top of them. When the truck groaned to a stop, Jessica's heart hammered so loudly, she was sure they would see the papayas on top of her moving.

Spencer heard the *federales* grilling Juan about where he was going and from where he'd come, asking if he'd seen anyone fitting Jessica's descriptions. Juan feigned ignorance and assured the *federales* he was just trying to get his papayas to market. At this, Spencer felt the side of the truck pull to one side as someone most likely looked in. Then the truck righted itself and a man yelled, "*Todo claro.*" Spencer exhaled.

Once the truck resumed driving, Juan soon hit higher speeds, until it was clear to Spencer they could sit up. Hopefully that was the last road-block until they arrived at their destination.

About a half hour later, Spencer spied resorts in the distance—where Annika sat in wait. He had to think quickly about their next move, for any wrong step could be fatal.

There was no other way to do this than to separate momentarily. They were looking for them as a unit. This was their best chance at getting back into their room undetected.

Jessica sat up and looked at him expectantly.

"When we get to the hotel, we should separate for a short time, since the reports are looking for us together," he said. "We can meet up at our room. They've got the credit card, so they're probably just continuing to charge it for each night."

Jessica's eyes were wide as she answered reluctantly, "I understand."

"You still have your key?"

She nodded.

When Juan pulled to the side of the road near the hotel, Jessica felt relieved she'd be getting out from amongst the papayas. She had a few orangey-yellow stains on her clothing and smelled of the fruit. Standing, she unearthed her bag and Spencer took it, along with his. He threw them onto the road and then helped her climb over the side of the truck. Juan wished them safe travels and then got in his truck and pulled away.

They stood at the foot of the long drive leading to the oceanside resort. The drive was lined with dense rows of palm trees on both sides. Spencer pointed to the left where the vegetation was thicker, and they headed that direction.

As they walked, they said nothing to one another, but Jessica imagined that Spencer's mind was pinging from one thought to another. She knew he was trying to figure out their next move. If she knew more about this Annika woman, she could help better. Maybe when they got back to the room, he would give her some more information about her.

When they neared the hotel, they stopped and hid in some shrubbery as they scoped out the entrance. "I say we leave our things here for now," said Spencer. "We can come back for them later."

Jessica started to protest, but he interrupted her. "It's a precaution, in case they stop us to take us in. Just walk in with your room key and your fake passport and stick like hell to being Joslyn Parker."

They put both their belongings under the shrubbery, pulling leaves and branches on top.

"You go first," he said. "Walk through the front doors like it's nothing and get to the room without attracting attention. They're looking for a blonde, so you should be okay."

Jessica turned to Spencer, willing herself not to show the fear coursing through her body. She must have done a poor job at hiding her hesitancy, because Spencer responded by pulling her to him and reassuringly stroking the back of her head as she nestled into his chest. "I'll be following right behind you, love, you'll be fine. Go on."

Any reply she might have uttered got stuck in Jessica's throat as she nodded, then she gazed into his eyes, which were clear and forthcoming.

"If something happens to me, I've put the name of someone in your phone at the Secret Service. Call the number. He'll come and get you."

Jessica's heart lurched at the thought of anything happening to Spencer, and she started to protest at his words, but he put a finger to her lips, and uttered, "You can do this."

She nodded, and he smiled.

Before she changed her mind, Jessica kissed Spencer on the lips, then turned and headed out of the trees, her head held high, willing herself to keep a steady gait. Breathe, Jessica, she reminded herself as she walked toward the doors of the hotel. Slow and steady. When she pushed open the door, the cool air from the hotel interior greeted her. Focus on the little details, she told herself. That would keep her distracted enough that before long she'd be in the room, safe, with Spencer. She calmly walked through the lobby with no incident and was rounding the corner for the elevators, when she saw Spencer enter the lobby in her peripheral vision. Just then, Mexican police officers were running towards him, shouting, "*Para! Federales!*"

Jessica flattened her body against the wall by the elevators so she couldn't be seen from the lobby. Straining to hear, she heard Spencer's deep voice talking to them in Spanish. He sounded calm, but then he always did. After a few agonizing moments where she didn't dare to breathe, she heard, "*Vamos al estación.*"

Jessica took a quick glance around the corner to see the officers leading Spencer out in handcuffs.

23

Jessica pushed the up arrow and stepped inside the empty elevator. Jabbing the third-floor button, she leaned against the wall as the elevator rose toward her floor. Once it stopped, she hurried out and made her way to the room. Praying the keycard would work, she slid it through. Relief poured through her body when it flashed green, and she pushed the door open.

Stepping cautiously inside, she surveyed the suite. Nothing appeared out of order. The bed was made, so the maid had been there. Otherwise, all looked just like they'd left it two days before. She dragged a chair to the corner and climbed up, pushing the ceiling tile back. Her computer was still there. She put the tile back in place and left the computer in hiding while she debated what to do next.

Maybe she should call Anthony. But what could he do from DC? The same went for Spencer's contact he put in her phone. He was also likely located in DC. Or she could find Annika in the hotel herself and lead the authorities to her. Then everything would be explained, and Spencer could be let free.

"Oh, God," Jessica said aloud, sitting on the edge of the bed and putting her head in her hands as the tears flowed. She let them spill for a minute, then stopped herself. Get it together, she thought. Sitting in the hotel room crying was a waste of time. It wasn't going to help her or Spencer.

After some thought, she decided to wait until nightfall and go and get their bags out of the shrubbery. Jessica glanced at the clock on the bedside table. Four o'clock. It would be dark by nine. In the meantime, she was starving. A papaya would have been good right about now. She found a bag of nuts in the cupboard, along with the equivalent of Mexican top ramen, which would just have to do. There was a microwave in the kitchenette, so she prepared the soup and sat down and scarfed it down.

She spent the rest of her time considering various strategies for finding Annika and getting her to confess. All the plans seemed like long shots, but she didn't have any other options. She resolved to find the woman and put an end to this whole charade, once and for all.

Right before nine, Jessica dressed in dark pants and a shirt and splashed some cold water on her face. She put her passport and hotel key in her pocket and headed out of the hotel room. Walking through the hall, she kept her head down, remembering what Spencer said about cameras. She rode the elevator to the lobby and took a deep breath when the doors slid open. Waiting to enter was a couple looking as if they'd just come back from dinner. They were giggling at some inside joke, and the man held the woman close. As Jessica passed them, she longed for Spencer's strong embrace.

Jessica made it out of the hotel without incident, then headed toward the trees. When the valet suddenly called out to her, her heart started hammering in her throat. Thankfully a car drove up, and his attention was diverted. She took the opportunity to swiftly dip into the shadows of the palm trees. Glancing up at the sky, she noted the moon was half full. It lit up her way with a milky haze.

She hadn't been paying as much attention as she should have when she and Spencer hid the bags, but she did remember more or less where they were. After a bit of looking around, she recognized the mound of branches and leaves. As she reached down to push away the vegetation, something moved below. She stifled a yelp when a giant rat shot past her. Working quickly, she removed the branches and leaves and grabbed their bags. She slung hers over her shoulder and tucked his under her arm and turned to make her way back toward the hotel.

When Jessica arrived at the edge of the stand of trees, she stopped and surveyed the situation. The valet was all alone. Not good. She'd attract too much attention. She'd have to wait until someone arrived and he got occupied.

It didn't take long before a vehicle snaked its way up the drive. Jessica crouched down before it arrived at the top of the hill so that the headlights didn't illuminate her. She remained kneeling while the Maserati pulled up in front of the hotel. The valet ran around to the driver's side door. Jessica stood to take advantage of the commotion but caught her breath and stopped when she heard a Russian accent. The woman stepped out of the car, and Jessica caught a good glimpse of her. She was gorgeous, with sharp features and shoulder-length platinum hair. Though Jessica was seeing her from a distance, she looked to be in her early forties. That would jive with what Spencer had told her—that his stepmother was only a decade older than him. Jessica watched as the woman slinked toward the front door.

Nervous that she had just seen what looked like Annika, and that she'd just barely missed running into her, Jessica waited for at least fifteen minutes before considering heading for the hotel. Finally, another car came up and a family piled out of the vehicle, giving her the perfect cover. The valet didn't notice her this time. She kept her head down as she walked through the lobby, her peripheral vision on high alert. When she got to the elevator, she willed it to come down quickly after pushing the button. She waited as the safety of her room seemed so close and yet so far away.

Jessica rushed into the elevator and turned around to hit the button of her floor. Just as the elevator doors started to shut, Annika strode past with a man on her right. She only got a quick look at the back of him before the elevator doors closed. He looked distinctly familiar to Jessica.

24

As Jessica rode up to her room, the man's familiarity nagged at her. Making her way down the hall, she saw a room service cart across from her suite. There was half a sandwich on the plate. It looked untouched. Quickly, before she talked herself out of it, she grabbed the food and let herself into her room. Dropping the bags in the living room, she sat down and bit into the sandwich, refusing to consider germs. She needed fuel to think through her next move.

After finishing every last crumb of the tasty turkey club, she retrieved Spencer's bag from the floor. She hated to go through his personal effects, but she had to find Annika's number. Her only hope right now—and it was a long shot—was to confront Annika and get her to confess. She would try to record the confession.

Jessica unzipped the small leather bag, which held a surprising amount. She pulled out the dress shirt and slacks she'd seen him wear when they arrived, as well as some socks and his underwear. Memories of the hayloft flitted through her mind, and she put his shirt to her nose and inhaled the husky odor that was him. Setting the shirt down, she found his cell phone at the bottom of the bag, and his gun, which she carefully removed and set on the table. She hadn't ever seen a gun up close, let alone touched one.

Reaching in his bag again, she extracted a smaller leather bag containing what looked like toiletries. She unzipped it, peering inside to see a razor, which she hadn't seen him use yet, toothpaste, a toothbrush, and a comb. She was about to zip the case shut, when something glinted at the bottom of the bag. Curiosity getting the better of her, she reached in and pulled out a black onyx bracelet. She had noticed that he rubbed his left wrist sometimes—especially when he was nervous or upset. Why wasn't he wearing this bracelet? She held it up under the lamp and examined it. The beads were worn. It was likely some years old. Jessica brought the bracelet to her lips and kissed it gently. Then she slipped it over her left wrist. She felt the need to keep it safe for him.

Next, she flipped open his phone, happy to see that it used the same charger as hers, as the battery was weak. She searched briefly until she came to a phone number that was labeled with an A. That had to be Annika.

Putting a chair under the ceiling tile, she stood on it, reaching up for and pulling down her computer and IMSI to hear conversations. Then she went to the table and opened her computer and plugged everything in. Hopefully it wasn't a long wait until Annika used her cell phone. Jessica went to the refrigerator, which still had a few sodas, and pulled one out.

Sitting back down, she waited with the frequency tuned to Annika's cell phone number. As soon as a call came through, she'd be there to listen —and hopefully discover her room number.

As the time passed, Jessica thought about turning on the television, but decided against it. She didn't want to get distracted. Besides, only one thing kept running through her mind, and that wasn't going to stop. Spencer. How was he? Was he safe? He'd warned her about Mexican jails, and now he was in one himself.

It was a good hour before there was any activity on Annika's cell phone. When it rang, Jessica jumped in the chair, then turned the volume up, as her connection was spotty.

"Are you with him?" A woman with a Russian accent asked.

"Yes. The fool has passed out again from too much alcohol."

"It's time to come home, my pet. You've got what you wanted. The authorities have Spencer."

"No, I haven't gotten what I want," Annika sneered. The tone in her voice jolted Jessica in her seat. "For one, I'm not finished with this one. How dare he fall asleep on me before I'm satisfied for the night. And then it's not the authorities who are supposed to have Spencer. It's me. We have unfinished business. And there's that woman he's with."

"What about her? She was merely a pawn. Isn't she also in custody?"

"No, she's missing. And I have it on good authority that she is not to be trifled with. She may look like a marshmallow, but her cyber skills are unrivaled. Pity, really, as I wanted to use her skills for a bit before disposing of her. I haven't been able to find a hacker worth their salt to get the information back home."

"Return to Russia, A. I will satisfy you more than any man ever could. I always do."

"I will be home in good time, like I always am. Keep the affairs in order there. I must go. The idiot is stirring."

When Annika hung up her cell phone, Jessica realized she'd been breathing in short bursts. Spencer had said he wanted to find his stepmother and end something; obviously she wanted the same.

Jessica strummed her fingers on the table. What was her next move? If only she knew the woman's room number. Then she could make her move. Jessica checked the time. It was nearly one in the morning. Most likely, Annika would soon be sleeping, but Jessica was willing herself to stay up all night. Eventually, Annika would give her room number to someone. And Jessica would be waiting.

At three in the morning, Jessica's eyelids were so droopy from listening to silence that she decided to lie down on the bed. She turned the volume on the computer to its max and soon fell into a fitful sleep. Visions of Spencer being led away in handcuffs drifted through her mind as she slept. Then Annika invaded her dreams, standing and aiming a gun at Spencer's head as Jessica watched. In the early morning hours, she woke to the sound of voices. Scrambling out of bed, she went to the computer, her ears on high alert.

"Mr. Rodrigo?"

"Yes."

"I hope you have the latest documents ready."

"I stayed up all night making them."

"Good."

"You said this is the last batch, right? I need to get home after this."

"You know what I like less than weak men, Mr. Rodrigo?"

Silence on the other end of the line. Finally, Rodrigo replied, "What?"

"Whiny, sniveling men. They make me want to use my gun."

More silence.

"Are you there, Mr. Rodrigo?"

"I'm here. You want me to bring the documentation to you?"

"Yes, let's do that. I'm at the same hotel. Room 544."

"I'll be there within the hour."

"Make that a half an hour, or you and your girlfriend will never have the children you've been promising her."

25

Jessica brewed some of the hotel coffee and then pulled up YouTube and typed in, "How to fire a gun." She was astounded to see there were actually instructional videos on the subject. As she sipped her coffee, she watched one.

Twenty minutes later, she put on Spencer's jacket, since she didn't have one of her own. She slid the gun into the back waistband of her pants as she'd seen people in movies do, including Spencer. Then she put her phone on record mode, so it would just take a poke of the button to record and slipped it into her bra. At the last second, she realized she hadn't put away her computer. Hurrying, she tucked it back above the ceiling tile, then hopped down from the chair, wincing when she remembered the gun at her back. She thought she'd put on the safety but wasn't sure. Carrying a weapon was going to take some getting used to.

She headed out of the room and hoped she wouldn't be too late. When she got to the fifth floor, she stole out of the elevator and peered down the hallway toward Annika's room. No one. Quietly making her way along the carpeting, she came to just before 544 and waited, noting that the door was slightly ajar. She heard voices inside and pressed her lips tight as she strained to listen.

"Mr. Rodrigo, if you want this to be quick and painless, just tell us where your workshop is, so we can go close it up. You've worn out your welcome, as the Americans say. Time to tie up loose ends, and you are one of the loosest." She snickered at her own joke.

"No need to end this. I can still be very useful," said Rodrigo.

"That's what men always say when they're completely useless. Jose, go ahead."

Realizing that she was just about to hear an execution, Jessica jumped over to the door and kicked it open, then aimed the gun at the scene in the room. Rodrigo was down on his knees with a gun trained on him. Annika looked up, surprise registering on her face. Then she smirked.

"Hold on, Jose, things just got a little more interesting."

"Let him go, or I'll pull the trigger," said Jessica, willing herself to hold the gun firmly, recalling the instructions on steady shooting she'd just seen on the video.

"Have you ever shot a gun?" Annika laughed, a bitter nail-to-chalk-board sound.

"I can and I will," said Jessica. "I'm not going to stand here and watch you shoot a man."

Annika laughed even louder. "Mr. Rodrigo is far from innocent. Okay, I'll play. So what are you doing here?"

"I've come for my social security number, and to stop you. You kill this man, and the authorities will also have you on murder charges."

"I've been told about your naivete, and to be frank, I thought it was a ruse. But I see now it may not be. My, what an innocent lamb you are. You know what happens to innocent lambs? They get slaughtered."

Jessica's mind whirled. Who had been talking to Annika about her? A strong arm suddenly reached from behind Jessica and grabbed the gun from her grasp, then shoved her into the room and slammed the door.

"Roberto. About time you got back. I was going to get rid of our friend, Rodrigo, but I need to tie them both up while I think this through."

Despite the early hour, Annika was smartly dressed in a black dress business suit. Her hair was wound into a chignon that rested at the back of her slender neck, offsetting diamond teardrop earrings.

The man named Roberto yanked Jessica onto a chair, then swiftly tied her hands to the back of it and secured her ankles to the rungs. He pulled a handkerchief out of his back pocket and motioned to put it in her mouth, but Annika stopped him.

"Not yet. Ms. Reynolds and I have some talking to do. You can rope up Mr. Rodrigo, though, like the pig he is. And do stuff that thing in his mouth. I've heard enough from him to last many lifetimes."

Roberto tied up Rodrigo and left him on the floor in what looked like an uncomfortable position as Jessica looked on, eyes wide.

"Before you say anything about that pig man there, I would reconsider." Annika warned her. "I can just as easily have you tied up in an unpleasant way."

Jessica remained mute, her eyes on Annika.

"Now," Annika turned her attention to Jessica. "Let's talk about how you know Mr. Rodrigo. Then we'll have a little chat about my favorite stepson."

Jessica didn't say anything.

"Are you mute?" Annika came to tower over Jessica. She was a tall woman. "Speak. How do you know Mr. Rodrigo?"

Annika's glowering gaze told Jessica she better respond.

"I only met him the other night," Jessica started. "He made a passport for me."

"Oh, really. And you did this all by yourself?"

Jessica nodded.

"How did you find out about Mr. Rodrigo?"

"A friend."

"Would that friend be my long-lost stepson?"

"I don't know who you're talking about." Jessica looked away as the woman grabbed her face and tilted her head up. Annika's eyes narrowed. "Don't bother trying to protect him. You might think he cares for you, but he doesn't. Spencer is in it for Spencer. I assure you."

Annika laughed again, her laugh grating on Jessica. Certainly, this woman was daft. After all, she was an identity thief and murderer. She was bound to say just about anything.

"Where is he, little lamb?" Annika's tone then turned icier. "I will find him. Since he wasn't answering his dear stepmother's calls, I had to do something drastic. I admit it's been fun impersonating Jessica Reynolds." She put her fingers on the diamonds hanging from her ears. "Thanks for these, by the way. They're divine. There was just enough credit left on your card."

Jessica scowled but was afraid to speak. Annika leaned closer to her face until Jessica could feel her breath on her own skin.

"How about we make a deal? You tell me where my stepson is, and I let you live so you can spend years paying off everything I put on your credit cards."

Just then Rodrigo attempted to speak. Irritated, Annika went over and dug her heel into his stomach, and he moaned. "I didn't ask you to talk."

She swung around and faced Jessica again. "I'm tiring of this conversation. How about I butcher this pig right in front of you, and you watch him bleed out on the carpet? You know what I want, and you best tell me."

"Or you'll what?"

Annika admired her manicure, and then replied, "Well, unfortunately, because of your cyber skills, I'm not able to lay a hand on your pretty head—at least not yet. But I can easily have the pig there killed."

This woman was psychotic. Jessica could tell she meant every word. She couldn't bring herself to be responsible for anyone's death. Maybe she could satisfy Annika with partial information, or false information.

"I'll tell you where he is," she blurted out.

Annika smiled; eyes full of interest. "Go on."

"He went to find us a way out of here. He's meeting someone in the plaza about chartering a boat."

Annika clapped her hands. "Very good, Ms. Reynolds, that's all you had to do. Roberto, you're with me. Jose, stay behind and watch over these two. We'll see if you're telling the truth, Ms. Reynolds."

They left the room, and Jessica's head swam. What was she going to do when Annika returned without her prey?

26

Spencer had pissed away several hours. His fake passport had checked out. He knew they suspected him of something, but they couldn't pin anything legit on him. The lead detective, Ruiz, even made a call to US Homeland Security. To Spencer's immense relief, one of his buddies answered and assured the officer his alias had no flags on the passport.

Spencer's biggest worry right now was Jessica. He had a nasty feeling she might go after Annika on her own. That thought made him frantic to get out of this God forsaken station. If Annika did anything to her, it would unravel him.

The interrogation room was a shithole with grimy gray walls. He sat at a cheap foldup table on a wooden chair. He was absolutely starving, and thirsty.

The door flung open then, and in stepped Ruiz, a scowl on his face, and another officer, tall and reedy with pockmarks on his face. He held a coke in his hands and smiled at Spencer as he announced, *"Hola, amigo!* Soy Lt. Guerro. You look like one of my relatives, but you say you aren't *Mexicano?"*

This shit again. Spencer silently seethed.

"Not that I know of, chap, but who knows. Perhaps one of my relatives in England took a secret trip to Mexico?"

That comment didn't sit well with Guerro, who pulled up the folding chair opposite Spencer and sat down, his smile turning to a frown, and his eyes morphing to steel.

Spencer kept his gaze trained on the officer, avoiding looking at the soda. He knew this ploy—get detainees as thirsty and hungry as possible and then dangle drinks and food for answers.

"You are quite a tough *hombre*, no? You've been here, what, sixteen hours without any nourishment?" The man looked down at the soda, but Spencer kept his eyes raised.

"I'm just a coffee importer, *Señor*. Checking out coffee of the region," repeated Spencer. They'd already had a coffee lover grill him on the various blends.

"So, you prefer coffee over soda?" said the officer, who pulled the tab on the can, sending the scent of cola into the air.

"I prefer to leave now that we've discussed my life story."

The officer leaned back and took a long drink. He wiped his mouth with the back of his hand when he finished and made a big show of enjoying it.

Spencer remained staring straight into the officer's eyes, refusing to react.

"*Hijole, hombre*. Okay, let me talk to *el capitan* and see if we can get you back to your coffee importing, of course."

Jessica tried to wriggle her hands free from the rope and was making progress. With time, she could probably break loose. But how many more minutes before Annika came storming back?

Rodrigo moaned on the floor again, and Jessica's eyes flew to him. She looked up at the guard. "Can you at least take the cloth out of his mouth?" The guard gave her a blank look and went back to staring straight ahead. Did he speak English, she wondered?

Jessica tried a different tactic. "I'm very thirsty. Could you help us?"

The guard glanced at her again, then motioned to pick up a cup from a bureau.

"I haven't had anything to eat or drink for hours. Perhaps you could get a soda from the vending machine? It's right down the hall."

The guard looked back and forth from her to Rodrigo. Then he shrugged. "You stay."

"No problem with that," Jessica said brightly.

Once he left the room, she swung her legs around to Rodrigo. "Watch out. I'm going to try to remove your gag with my feet." A couple of swipes, and he was able to spit it out.

"I have a knife in my back pocket," he said, his voice raspy. "If you can get to it."

Just then the key entry on the door beeped. Rodrigo grabbed the cloth back up with his mouth and lay there still.

The guard walked in with a soda, and Jessica exclaimed. "Oh, thank you! Although, I might need a little help to drink it."

He popped the tab and went up to Jessica, putting the can up to her mouth. She gulped several mouthfuls. "That's good for now. You're very kind."

Setting the can down, he went back to his post, staring into space while Jessica secretly worked on getting her hands free.

When Spencer finished signing the last of the blasted paperwork for his release, he stormed out of the station and onto the street. It was bright outside—and hot. His head swam for a second, and he realized he absolutely needed liquid. During a break in traffic, he crossed the busy street and felt like kissing a street vendor when he saw she had bottled water. He bought a big bottle and downed it right then and there.

He hoped Jessica was safely holed up in the hotel room as he cut through the plaza to get there quicker. While walking, out of the corner of his eye, he spotted a tall blonde. Dear God! Annika. He quickly ducked behind a building. She was talking to someone and appeared agitated, but he soon lost sight of her as a large group of tourists crossed their path. Spencer took the chance to rush onto the street toward the hotel.

Jessica finally worked her hands free. Trying not to raise suspicion, she kept them behind her back and started to squirm in her chair.

The guard looked at her, annoyed.

"I need to use the bathroom," she said. "Can you let me loose? Just for a minute."

"Not without permission."

"Well, can you call your boss? You can stand outside the door the whole time. I really have to go."

The guard shook his head, then shrugged his shoulders and went into an adjacent room of the suite to make the call. Quickly, she untied her feet and ran over to Rodrigo, pulling the knife out of his back pocket and cutting the ties binding him. He jumped to his feet, and she gave him the knife. They heard the guard finishing his call with Annika. Rodrigo motioned for Jessica to sit back down, then he stood out of sight. When the guard entered, Rodrigo jumped him from behind and they began struggling. It looked like at one point the guard was going to stab Rodrigo in the face, but the knife ended up in the guard's gut. As he fell over onto the bed, Rodrigo shouted, "*Vámonos!*" and sped out of the door.

Jessica sprang to her feet, hesitating for a moment as she watched the guard writhe in pain on the bed. Then she turned and ran—straight into the broad chest of Roberto with Annika behind him.

27

"Where are you going, stupid little lamb?" Annika said as Roberto drug her back into the room, depositing her in the chair. Annika shut the door and glanced at the spot where Rodrigo had been lying, and then looked at her guard, who lay gasping from the knife in his stomach.

She turned to Jessica. "Look at all the trouble you've caused. Roberto, get rid of him—in the bathroom for now. Then go find that idiot, Rodrigo. I'm fine here with my new friend while we wait for my stepson to arrive." She gave Jessica a grin that sent a cold lump plummeting to the bottom of her stomach.

Roberto nonchalantly took his gun and shot the other guard in the chest. He waited for a moment, and Jessica watched in horror as the man's body shuddered. Roberto then wrapped him in the bedspread and hoisted his body over to the bathroom, where Jessica heard him dump the man with a thud in the bathtub. The bathroom door closed; Roberto left the hotel room.

Annika pulled up a chair across from Jessica. She sat down, crossing one long, elegant leg over the other and smoothing her skirt.

"Isn't this cozy," Annika said. "This will give us time to get to know one another. And for me to tell you a few stories about my stepson."

When Spencer arrived at the hotel, he rushed through the front doors and to the elevator. He willed himself to calm down and strategize, but he barreled out of the elevator on the third floor, almost knocking over a mother and her child waiting to step on.

"*Disculpame*," he apologized, taking long strides down the hall. He arrived at their room and slid the card through, pushing the door open when the green light blinked.

"Jessica," he called out. There was only silence. He saw his bag on the table, along with hers, so she had made it to the room. Bloody hell. Where was she?

"You look uncomfortable. Did I say something that disturbs you? About my stepson, perhaps?"

"No."

"Hmm." Annika leaned forward, piercing Jessica's eyes with hers. Though she was repulsed by the woman, Jessica didn't flinch.

"Spencer is quite a dish to look at, wouldn't you say?"

Jessica shrugged. "I guess so."

"You're not fooling me with your nonchalant attitude, my lamb." Annika leaned back in her chair. Her smile had turned to stone. "Perhaps Spencer hasn't told you about us." Her eyes were slits that reminded Jessica of the snake she'd killed the other day. "I've seen that look before on many women's faces when it comes to Spencer. You've fallen for him. Don't be ashamed about it. Many do, and they have no idea what a bad idea that is."

Jessica felt a fury with this woman like none she'd ever felt before. Was that what hate felt like? Every fiber in her body burned with disdain.

"I know Spencer. I know what's in his heart."

Annika laughed again. "Oh, do you? Do you also know that he's responsible for his mother's demise?"

It was Jessica's turn to laugh. "Explain to me how a young boy caused his mother to become mentally ill?"

"I see he's told you a thing or two about himself. That's a first."

"Yes, we've talked. About his mother. And about you." At the interest that flicked into Annika's eyes with Jessica's last remark, she soon regretted mentioning that part.

"Oh, really. Do tell. I'm all ears."

"Never mind."

"If it was about me, I'd like to know what dear Spencer said."

"He didn't say anything. Just that you were his stepmother."

"Did he tell you about us?"

Jessica felt a slither of unease race up and down her spine.

"What about you? That you were married to his father?"

Annika grinned. "I see he didn't tell you everything, after all."

"He told me how you had his mother committed, and how that killed her."

"That woman should have been committed years before I met his father. She would have made Spencer as loony as she was at the rate she was going." Annika looked at the burgundy polish on her manicured nails.

"Bipolar disorder isn't contagious." Jessica felt the need to defend Spencer and the mother he loved so much.

"No, but it is hereditary," replied Annika. "Although as intimately as I know my dear stepson, he isn't at all like his mother in that department."

Spencer looked around the hotel room hoping to find some clue as to where Jessica could have headed. No cell phone—just clothing and toiletries. Then he remembered the computer. Pulling a chair over, he pushed the ceiling tile out of the way and removed the computer. Bringing it to the table, he powered it up, smiling when Jessica's screen-saver came up. A white, furry cat stared back at him.

He checked her recent search history but blast it all if he could make any sense of it. He was completely out of his league when it came to higher-level computer operations. Spencer was just closing the computer, when the hotel room door eased open. He turned, relief washing through him. But it wasn't Jessica. Rodrigo entered and shut the door.

"What the hell are you doing here, and where is Jessica?"

"That Russian *loca* has her. She dropped her key, and I nabbed it. They gave me the room number at the front desk when I showed it to them."

"Now I'm really starting to lose patience," said Annika. "I was trying to do this the nice way."

She stood up and went to a bureau by the bed, extracting a knife with a sharp tip that made Jessica cringe. "A little steel to skin with my trusty knife here, and I think you'll soon be telling me where Spencer is."

Annika came toward Jessica with the knife, a glint in her eyes that set Jessica's teeth on edge. She stopped in front of Jessica, placing the tip of the blade on her finger and giving it a twirl. The knife must have cut her skin, because her finger started to bleed. She looked at it absentmindedly and then sucked the blood from her finger.

"Don't worry, little lamb. I won't start with areas of your body that are visible." Annika reached over and pulled up Jessica's blouse as she recoiled from her. There was a rapping on the door just then.

"It's me. Open up."

Annika sighed and set the knife on the bed. She walked to the door, calling out, "Darling, I thought you'd never get back." When she pulled it open, Jessica gaped. Anthony, her boss, stood there.

28

Annika snaked herself around Anthony, giving him a kiss on the mouth. Then he noticed Jessica in the chair.

"What the hell is she doing here?" He strode into the room with that irritated edge to his voice Jessica knew so well.

Annika closed the door and stroked Anthony's arm. He wore one of his ultra-expensive suits and the wing-tipped shoes he loved. Jessica had always wondered how he could afford such a wardrobe, and all the fancy trips he took.

"It couldn't be helped, darling," Annika said. "Sorry. I know she is an important asset."

"She's my only asset at this point." Anthony thundered, but Annika didn't move a muscle. "You never realized we need her to get the social security numbers to your friends in Russia, and to make deposits to our overseas account?"

"We can make a visit to her family, if she doesn't cooperate."

Anthony turned to Jessica, who sat speechless, but managed to sputter, "That's what you had me doing all this time? I wasn't looking for fraud. I was committing it." She was horrified.

Her boss shook his head. "Always the goody two-shoes. I sure as shit won't miss that. If it helps your conscious, doll, most of that was corporate espionage."

Anthony snorted then and turned back to Annika. "You got any scotch to drink?"

"Of course, your favorite." She strode over to the minibar, humming under her breath.

"Where are all your goons?"

"Roberto is out dealing with some loose ends. Jose suffered an unfortunate demise. His body is in the bathroom." She handed Anthony a drink and held up hers. They clinked glasses.

"So what are we doing waiting around?" he said after gulping his drink down in one swallow. "Get me another one," he demanded, shoving the glass into her hand.

Annika went to the bar to mix him another drink. After he grabbed it and took another long gulp, he asked, "How long is your reunion with Spencer going to take?"

"Not long. Just my final score. Then Roberto will clean up the mess." Annika checked a thin diamond-studded watch on her wrist. "I don't think it will be much longer. You gave Spencer the job of looking after this waif for a sizeable chunk of cash. He'll come to find her and get his payout. Of course, he has no idea what's really going on, but he will soon enough."

What was really going on? Jessica so wanted to know. It was clear that Anthony was using her as usual—this time to lure Spencer to Annika. But Jessica felt like she was missing a big piece of the puzzle here.

"I can see the wheels turning," Annika said to Jessica. "Yes, dear, you mean nothing to Spencer than a big paycheck. I assure you."

"For God's sake, the deadline is approaching for getting the information to Russia," Anthony announced. "Your reunion with your stepson might have to wait."

"We still have time." Annika waved toward Jessica. "Why don't you get her ready."

Anthony extracted a laptop from his bag and opened it, setting it on the desk. He powered it on and tapped in his password. "You got the flash drive?" he asked Annika.

"Of course." She dug around in her purse and pulled out the device, handing it to him.

He placed it next to the computer, then gestured to Jessica. "Get the data off this thing and into an encrypted email. I want to bounce off at least twenty cell towers when you send it. More insurance we won't get caught while we're getting out of town."

Anger overcame Jessica at the man's audacity. "Do it yourself."

Anthony stood up, the look on his face a seething volcanic rage that threatened to overflow. Jessica had never seen this side of him before, because she'd always said yes. Well, those days were over.

"The way I see it," Spencer told Rodrigo, "You owe Jessica. If it wasn't for you using her social to make fake cards, she'd be safe at home right now."

"I told you, *hombre*, the Russian woman threatened to ice me and my girlfriend if I didn't do it."

"Annika wants me. We have a score to settle."

"Yeah, well, she was just referring to me as a loose end."

"Didn't you say Jessica helped you escape?"

"I'm telling you! That woman is scary!"

"Believe me. I know. This is your chance to get her put behind bars."

"Yeah, and maybe me, too. I've got some warrants out for my arrest."

"I'll put in a good word for you. I've got friends in high places."

"*Chinga*," Rodrigo muttered, pacing the small room "Okay, what do you want me to do? And what about her partner?"

"What partner?" That stopped Spencer. "What do you mean?"

"Big, tall guy with fancy clothing. He's there sometimes when I drop off documents. He's not one of her goons."

"You know his name?"

Rodrigo concentrated a moment.

All the pieces fell together right in front of Spencer then. "Is his name Anthony?" he asked Rodrigo.

Rodrigo's eyes lit up. "Yeah, that's it."

Things just became clearer to Spencer—and he knew exactly how to handle them now.

"Don't say no to me." Anthony's voice was low and threatening as he leaned down, putting his face in Jessica's. She nearly gagged at the odor of alcohol and cigarettes on his breath.

"Or what? You're going to fire me?" she said, unwilling to let this bully of a man have his way anymore.

"I've got people, Jessica. You know that. We know your parents' home isn't far out of DC." He let his words hang in the air. "I can have someone there in thirty minutes."

"What are you going to do to them?" Jessica tried not to react, but fear for their safety filled her with alarm.

"Nothing, if you do what you're told. Now get over there and get the computer ready to transmit those documents." He pulled her out of the chair and pushed her toward the desk. "It's all on the flash drive."

Then she saw him out of the corner of her eye go to the bar and pick up the empty bottle of scotch. "Where's the rest of it, dar—ling." He drew out the last word.

Nerves teetering on the edge, Jessica tried to focus on the screen as she stuck the flash drive in the computer and watched the files come up. She wracked her brains for what to do next. Anthony didn't have her level of computer skills, but he would know if she sent the data. So busy was Jessica trying to think her way out of this mess that it took a moment for the grunt of pain behind her to register. Swinging around, she screamed to see Annika standing over Anthony as he fell to his knees on the floor, the empty scotch bottle in his grasp and a knife in his chest.

"You are such a lush," Annika said, her voice dripping with contempt. "My skin crawled every time we were together. I've finally got the files, and I can finally get rid of you. Spencer will soon be here, and we'll go and enjoy the Cayman's together."

Anthony gave one final groan and fell on the carpeting. Annika smiled as if patting herself on the back, then turned her attention back to Jessica. "I do hope you're doing your work there. I would hate to have to send someone to your parents' home in Virginia. Fairfax, isn't it? On Crescent Avenue?"

Jessica turned back to the computer, grasping at what to do. Annika likely planned to kill her after she completed the task. But if she didn't, she'd have her parents killed.

"Why are you just sitting there? I'm getting irritated, and when I get irritated, people get hurt."

"Obviously," said Jessica dryly. If she was going to die, she wasn't going to go down easy. "I'm working on your precious files." She began replacing the files with innocuous ones, tapping away with concentration.

"No tricks, lamb. My associates in Russia will check the files as soon as they arrive and get back to me if they aren't correct."

Just then there was a rap on the door. Annika went to peer through the peephole, then opened the door with a flourish. "There you are!" she exclaimed.

29

Spencer strode into the room and appeared to welcome Annika's embrace.

"It's been way too long, my dear," Annika said, devotion in her eyes as she stroked his face.

"That it has," said Spencer, glancing over at Anthony. "I see you got rid of him. How am I going to get my money now?"

Annika grinned at Jessica. "See, I told you. He has no interest in you. Only money, and his dear stepmother, of course." She turned her attention back to Spencer. "I've so dreamed of our reunion. But you have some explaining to do."

Spencer avoided eye contact with Jessica and smiled at Annika. "You mean why I shot you and ran after father died?"

"Yes, that," Annika said coyly. "I do love rough play, but that was a bit over the top."

"Father's money."

"What do you mean?"

"If I stayed with you, I wouldn't have gotten anything from the estate. The money was in a trust until last month. We're free to be together now."

"And all this time I thought you were angry with me about talking your father into putting your crazy mother into that home."

Jessica watched Spencer's jaw tighten at that comment, and she tried to make eye contact with him. His hand went suddenly to his wrist. Instinctively, Jessica touched the bracelet on her arm. The movement caught Spencer's eye, and he looked at Jessica in shock. Annika noticed the exchange immediately.

"Liar," she yelled, picking up her knife and wielding it in his face. "You think you can play me? I saw how you looked at her."

Spencer visibly reigned in his emotions. "I care for her like I might care for a pet. I'm not a stupid man, Annika. I know the files you're sending to Russia probably contain thousands of social security numbers and personal information that's going to earn us millions."

Annika hesitated, clearly thinking through what Spencer just said. Then, she replied, "I have no idea what files you're talking about."

"The files you have on the computer there for Jessica to transmit."

"Anthony gave her those files. I don't know what they are. I'm just here on vacation minding my own business."

"Using Jessica's identify while you do so."

"I had no idea that the information I got from Mr. Rodrigo was fake. I thought he was making me a passport."

So this is how Annika was going to play it. Damnit all. Rodrigo had gone to the police station to alert the authorities, who would be here any minute. Spencer had to get her confession as soon as possible, or she'd slip out of Interpol's grasp as she usually did.

"Who killed Anthony?" he asked.

"I had to defend myself."

"I doubt Jessica saw it that way."

"Stop looking at her." Annika said coolly. "Don't you understand that when you ignore me, people get hurt?"

"Like my mother?" Spencer had to keep it together. But how he wanted to strangle this woman.

"And all of those insipid girlfriends when you were growing up."

This was a new one to Spencer.

"Remember the skiing accident? And the car crash?"

Spencer was so overcome with fury, he felt like he was going to explode. This woman had plagued his life long enough. And he'd be damned if he'd let her harm Jessica.

"What if I proved my loyalty to you?" he said, matching her even tone.

"Explain." Annika crossed her arms.

"Jessica transmits the files, then we ensure the payout. Afterwards, I'll finish her off, and we're out of here."

Annika's eyes glittered with suspicion. "You would do that for me?"

Spencer nodded. He stalked over to Jessica and ordered, "Transfer those files." He turned to Annika, "Where do they go?"

"Moscow. Payout is forty-five million."

The words were still coming out of her mouth when the door burst open and Mexican police flooded in. The pockmarked Lt. Guerro, along with a few of his police buddies, grabbed Annika as she tried to climb out the hotel window. It took three of them to wrestle her to the floor kicking and biting, a stream of expletives spewing from her mouth. Arms behind her back, fists balled up, the lieutenant handcuffed her. Then they immobilized her legs with a restraint, taking no chances when it came to the notorious Annika Morozov.

When she was contained, Lt. Guerro looked up at Spencer, laughing. "Damn *hombre*, you're a little bit of everywhere. I apologize. We didn't know you were on our side. Looks like with your help we have a chance for a solid case against this woman."

"You betrayed me," Annika cried, spitting in Spencer's direction. "You stupid man. All that money, the yachts, the villas and jewels to waste!" The officers lifted Annika to her feet and dragged her out. At the last second, she turned and glared at Jessica with such hatred Spencer was relieved to know the woman would be locked away for a long time. Annika continued to screech as they moved her down the hall.

Spencer turned to Jessica, who had been watching, eyes wide. Relief swept through his body as they embraced. "You have no idea how worried I was about you," he said into her soft hair.

When they finally pulled apart, Jessica gazed into Spencer's eyes.

"I'm so sorry about Annika," he said. "It was me she was after all along. I knew when I was younger that she had a fascination with me, but I never expected it ran this deep. I always thought she hated me because I shot her."

"So you did shoot her?"

"Yes, I'm not proud of it. I had just found out that my father had died. They said a heart attack, but now I wonder about that. I was twenty-one at the time and confused and upset about my father passing. Then Annika had the nerve to tell me that it was best that my crazy mother and gambling addict father were dead. She had the gun out for some reason. She always had a fascination with weapons. I grabbed the gun, shot her in the arm and ran."

"Well, she's going away for a long time now," said Jessica.

"I hope so. Unfortunately, the lawyers will probably use the fact that I did shoot her against me and try to discredit my testimony about her confessions. They'll want to question you, too. But it's our word against hers. And Annika is legendary for slipping out of the authority's grasp."

"Wait!" Jessica cried. "It's not her word against ours. I've got it all on tape." She pulled her cell phone out of her bra.

"You are absolutely brilliant!" Spencer laughed and hugged her.

At the station, they separated Spencer and Jessica to take down their stories. In the end, the Interpol agent informed them that their recollections matched for the most part, and they were free to go. The cell phone recording Jessica had made would likely convict Annika.

"What will happen with her?" Spencer asked.

"This is the first time we've had her on record admitting to her offenses, and we thank you for that," the Interpol agent said, nodding to Jessica. "The murder charges alone will keep her in prison for decades."

Spencer and Jessica were totally free to leave the station. It was a balmy, beautiful night that under other circumstances would have inspired strolling along the bay, but the stress of the day had left Spencer exhausted.

"I don't know if I've ever been so tired in my life," Jessica echoed his thoughts.

He put his arm around her shoulders. "How about if we order room service and then call it a night?"

When they were eating dinner in their room an hour later, Spencer stared at the bracelet on Jessica's arm. She must have felt him looking at it, because she stopped and glanced down at her wrist.

"I was searching in your bag for anything that might help me find Annika. When I saw the bracelet, I felt sure it was important. I didn't want someone to find and take it. Your mother gave this to you, didn't she?"

Spencer nodded.

"You don't wear it, but you keep it with you? Why?"

Spencer ran his fingers through his hair and thought for a moment. It was time to be honest about his feelings. And honest with Jessica. She deserved that.

"I've tried to wear it many times, but for lack of a better way of saying this, it hurts too much. Even after all these years, the loss still seems so fresh. Maybe because I had no closure. But I could never get rid of the bracelet, so I carry it with me. This probably all sounds strange."

Jessica reached out and put her hand on his. "It makes perfect sense." She removed the bracelet from her arm and handed it to him. "Maybe you want to wear it now?"

Spencer grasped it in his hand. "I'll think about it."

30

Where on earth were they headed? Spencer wondered as they traveled into the countryside the next day. Jessica was at the wheel of a rental car she insisted they get. She refused to give him even a little hint. He had to admit that he enjoyed the intrigue. Even better, he enjoyed being with Jessica.

Finally, they drove down a winding, tree-lined drive toward a large building set on a handful of acres. A giant wooden sign nestled in the shrubbery read *Facilidad Mental de Cristo*. Jessica stopped the car, and Spencer looked out the window. "I'm confused. Why are we here?"

Jessica laid a hand on his arm. "We're here to visit someone."

"Okay. That is a relief. At least you're not dropping me off at the door."

Jessica laughed and climbed out of the car. "Let's go inside. They're expecting us."

Spencer and Jessica walked to the front door and entered. To the right was a check-in desk. When Jessica approached, the receptionist looked up and smiled.

"I'm Jessica Reynolds. I called this morning."

"Oh, yes, you made it. Wonderful. I'll be right back."

"Thank you." Jessica called after her, taking Spencer's hand in hers.

"You trust me, right?" she said quietly, looking at his wrist. He had put the bracelet from his mother on this morning.

The events of the last few days flashed through Spencer's mind. "Of course, I trust you."

She looked up at him, tears glistening in her eyes. "I hope you're not angry with me. I just thought this would be so good for you both."

Spencer shook his head, still mystified. "Us both?"

The head nurse arrived then, welcoming them with a wide grin. "So glad you could both come." She turned on her white nursing shoes and lead them a short distance to the facility's visiting room. "She is having an especially good day today," said the nurse as she opened the door. "Very aware and alert. So, this is perfect."

Spencer's mind struggled with what was about to happen. He looked at Jessica.

"She's here, Spencer. Your mother is still alive."

He hesitated as if unable to take the words in. He just stood there unsure what to do.

"I'll wait here," she said, encouraging him through the door.

Spencer nodded; his body numb. He followed the nurse to a woman sitting in a chair watching cartoons, her back to them. The nurse leaned over and spoke in her ear, and the woman began clapping as Spencer approached and went around to face her. He fell on his knees in front of his mother unable to speak.

"My Spencey!" she cried, overjoyed. "Mama knew you would come. I've been waiting for you."

He couldn't stop staring at her, kissing her hands. Surely this wasn't real, only a dream, he thought. How could his father have lied all those years to him? What Jessica would say whispered in his ear. Nothing else mattered except his mother was here now. Right here in front of him. He pressed his cheek against hers, then took her face in his hands. Though the lines were etched deep around her mouth and brow, she was as beautiful as ever, her long black hair woven with strands of silver.

"I didn't know you were here, Mama. They told me you had died. I'm so sorry. I'm so sorry." Years of pent-up tears flowed down his face, blurring his vision.

"It's okay, *mi cielo*! Mama knew you were busy, and now you are here." She wiped the tears from his face, and he looked into her eyes, which sparkled as they always had.

Spencer hugged her, the tears flowing as he melted into her embrace. Oh, God, how he had missed this all those years. He didn't realize until now just how much.

When he finally pulled away, his mother asked, "Can you stay for lunch, Spence? They are having my favorite. Tater tots and fish sticks." Her eyes gleamed with joy. "And then the salad that they make me eat." She made a funny face, and Spencer laughed.

"I would love to, Mama, if a friend of mine can come along."

"I'm so happy you have finally made a friend, Spence. I hope she likes tater tots!"

Jessica came to stand beside Spencer, and his mother gazed at her for a moment. "She is so beautiful, Spence, like that doll we used to play with, remember? The one with the blonde hair and blue eyes?"

Jessica's hands instinctively went to her hair. "I am actually naturally a blonde, and I plan to let this grow out."

"You're beautiful because you're you," his mother said simply. "That's what I always told Spencer, didn't I?"

Spencer's throat constricted at the memory. He'd forgotten about that. He nodded.

The nurse approached then and said, "Let's get everyone to lunch before all of the tater tots are gone."

As Jessica followed Spencer and his mother to the dining hall, she breathed a sigh of relief. It wasn't until now that she realized how stressed she'd been about this reunion being a good one, since she put the plan into motion. After Spencer relayed there was never a funeral, she wondered if there was any chance that his mother might still be alive. A little online sleuthing last night after he fell asleep and a few quick calls this morning while he was in the shower, and she was shocked to find out the truth. Angelica Abbott had been living in this home for the past sixteen years. Her care apparently funded by Spencer's father's estate. The nurses told Jessica that Angelica had spoken about Spencer many times, but they thought he was a figment of her imagination.

After an enjoyable lunch and much talk of Spencer's childhood, which delighted Jessica to hear, they left his mother, promising to return as soon as possible. They spoke to the nurses about transferring her to a facility in the United States now that Spencer could prove kinship. Spencer would be looking into that when they got back home.

As they exited the hospital, Spencer stopped and took Jessica's hands in his. He appeared truly mystified. "No one has ever done anything like this for me." He reached up and began caressing her hair, then almost whispered, "I don't want to live without you."

"Nor I you," Jessica replied, smiling one of her brilliant smiles.

"Does that mean what I think it means?"

She laughed. "I hope so. Although, there are a couple of things you'll need to be able to live with."

Spencer raised his eyebrows and waited.

"Cats and teddy bears." She smiled.

He took her in his arms, murmuring in her ear, "I knew they were part of the package."

EPILOGUE

Spencer and Jessica's stories are complete, but Tony's is just beginning...

Tony Molinaro set down the brew he'd been drinking and gazed at the Puerto Vallarta night sky. He liked to look for stars that blinked, because they were the ones that soon fell. Just about every night during dry season, he spotted at least one falling star. What he wished for, again and again, was the same thing: that Joanna would stop hating him and agree to talk.

"Damnit," he muttered under his breath, taking another long pull of the beer. Fact was, he was getting sick of this shit. Holed up out in the middle of the jungle by himself. His house was cool, and he was proud to have built it with his own hands, but he was sick as hell of being alone. Every time he tried to start something with someone, it fizzled. His feelings were still too wound up in Joanna, and the chicks could sense it. He didn't have to say one damn word.

The project he'd been working on kept him busy, though, and on his toes. So, most days he didn't think about his love life. The maudlin crap usually just happened when he sat outside, thinking.

Tony jumped when he heard a beep. His cell phone had sent out an alert code he set up in case of emergencies. Springing up, he ran inside and saw the words on his phone. Operation Ottoman Suspend Immediately. Just then, he heard a vehicle approaching—he never got company out here at night.

Nerves on overdrive, Tony popped open the case of his computer and removed the hard drive containing all his data. The vehicle's engine became louder as the blood pumped in his neck. He grabbed his go bag and ran to the back of the house. Taking a remote out of his pocket, he pressed open, and the wall slid back. He jumped inside and pressed close just as they stormed his home. Pulling out his cell, he lit up the stairs and ran down into the tunnel.

See what happens with Tony in *Discovered Betrayal*. Or better yet, check out the next four books in the series, starting with Tony's story: The Discovered Truth Series Box Set Books 5-8.

A NOTE FOR YOU

Dear Reading Gem,

Thanks for spending time with me, Spencer and Jessica! While each of the books in the Discovered Truth Series can be read as a standalone, it's fun to experience the progression and get to know the characters. The series progresses as minor characters introduced in each book become main characters in subsequent books. It's exciting to see what they'll do next!

The Discovered Truth series features complex, gutsy women and equally complicated, charismatic men who find themselves immersed in dangerous and intriguing modern-day challenges, such as human trafficking, drug and diamond smuggling, national security threats, and identity theft. When the heroine and hero meet, worlds collide and sparks fly, kindling unforgettable romance and intrigue.

If you like the series, please leave a review on any book review platform. Your opinion matters and is incredibly powerful.

Thanks again and talk soon!

STAY ENLIGHTENED

Thanks for reading! Let's stay in touch. In appreciation of you, I post updates, insider information, and sneak peeks of upcoming books on my website at https://www.juliebawdendavis.com/fiction. You can also email me at Julie@JulieBawdenDavis.com, follow me on Facebook, and find me on Amazon.

Even better, you can join my VIP Reading Gems mailing list here. I also created a Facebook group especially for you! Join Julie's Reading Gems to get the inside scoop on what's going on with the Discovered Truth Series. Find out how characters are created, and what they might do next. I also ask for Reading Gem opinions on character names. And there are lots of contests and giveaways!

Speaking of giveaways, download the prequel to the Discovered Truth Series, *Discovered Beginnings*, for FREE by clicking HERE.

Escape to Unforgettable Romance and Intrigue…

BOOKS IN THE DISCOVERED TRUTH SERIES

Box Sets

The Discovered Truth Series Box Set Books 1-4

The Discovered Truth Series Box Set Books 5-8

The Discovered Truth Series Box Set Books 9-12

The Discovered Truth Series Box Set Books 13-16